The Writer's Gift

**FOLLOW THE AUTHOR ON THESE SOCIAL MEDIA
SITES: Facebook: JUSTIN Q YOUNG
Periscope**: JUSTIN Q YOUNG
Twitter: OFFICIALAUTHORQ
Instagram: firstborn_design
Pinterest: JQYOUNG76

ITEMS CAN BE PURCHASED AT THE FOLLOWING:
www.firstborndesigns.com
www.mkt.com/firstborndesigns

ISBN:0692607099
ISBN-13:9780692607091

CONTENTS

FIRSTBORN DESIGNS

ACKNOWLEDGMENTS

I want to thank all of the contributing authors on this project.
I literally woke up one morning wanting to give back, made a
post about my idea online and that's how this project came
about.
The authors within these pages didn't hesitate or blink twice
when I said I wanted to donate all online proceeds to a non-
profit. Seasoned and up and coming alike, these authors are
amazing and I am thankful for their contributions, their time, and
their willingness to GIVE BACK!
May you all continue to see the success you want and be blessed
in your endeavors!

I also want to thank all of you who I have met or who have
supported me along the way. I take nothing for granted.

Without further ado, allow me to introduce to you, Nenaya
Renee, Sapphire James, Marie A. Norfleet, Kisha Green, Unique
Penn, Nikki P. Serene, M. Dawn, RR Moore, Candii,
Rasheemah, Honey Bee, Imani Ferrier, King Diamond, Tracey
McLean & Jodie Pierce

ROLE PLAY
By Nenaya Renee

My hips swayed to the beat, fingers tangled in my hair. Perspiration ran from my temples dissolving into my skin. I caught his gaze across the dance floor, scorching. He leaned back against the bar, crossed his ankles, and watched my every move.

"Can I have this dance?"

He was a stranger to me. His breath was hot against the base of my ear, dripping with sex. I shifted slightly to get a better look at him. He was young, handsome.

"Sure."

He splayed his hand across my belly drawing me into him, our bodies in sync with the rhythm. The mystery man kept his eyes on me biting at his lower lip, hot for me. My dance partner moved his hands to my hips forcing me to match his groove. A woman approached my mystery man, her hand pressed to his chest as she leaned into him. She said something that made his mouth curve up into a sly grin. Jealousy bubbled through me.

He pulled his eyes away to acknowledge her. They exchanged dialogue before she turned and walked away. His eyes were back on me enjoying the show the stranger and I were putting on. The mystery man downed the last of his drink and set the empty glass on the bar. He nodded his head toward the door slipping into the multitude of inebriated clubbers.

I turned around, offering the stranger a smile. "Thanks for the dance, handsome."

"Can I get your number?"

"I'm sorry love, I'm only here on vacation. It would never work." I didn't give him a chance to counter my rejection before rushing off toward the bathroom. Drunken and strident women trickled from the restroom in packs.

I leaned over the bathroom sink, applied a fresh coat of red lipstick to my full lips. I swept my hand over a few rebellious curls pushing them back into place, reached over snatching a fistful of napkins from the dispenser. I squinted, widened my eyes trying to bring my reflection into focus in the smudged mirror. Three...four...maybe five. I had lost count after the fourth drink. I was reeling, teetering back on my five inch black pumps.

I staggered clumsily gripping the counter for leverage. The song changed. The bass thumped loudly through the speakers rattling the walls, making the floor jump with its every beat.

"Get it together, Faith," I mumbled.

I drew in a deep breath, having convinced myself that I was put together enough to leave, I headed for the door. Men licked their lips like wolves preying on their next meal. Their eyes played over my curves, sexual invitations fell from their lips. I kept my eyes pinned to the crowd working my way through to the exit. Bodies were pressed together.

Women danced closely with men, some they probably didn't know before they got here. The heat that swelled up from the mass clung to my bare arms, saturating my dress as it pressed against my back. I stepped out into the cooling night air. The breeze whisked against my warm skin pulling me slightly out of my drunkenness. A languid smile crept across my face at the sight of him.

"I'm really doing this," I thought as I walked closer.

The sound of my heels against the pavement drew his attention to me. He wet his lips with his tongue in a way that sent a shiver coursing through my body. Maybe it was the chill that hung in the air or maybe it was the way my body craved him. He stuck his arm out into the street flagging down a taxi.

"For a minute, I thought you were just a tease," he breathed as I eased into his side, my nails traveling down the length of his spine.

"You want to get out of here?"

I looked up at him through lustful eyes shaking my head with consent. A cab halted at the curb, waited as we climbed inside. His cologne was as intoxicating as the liquor drumming through my veins. My ears swam with the echoes of the music from the club. I heard him tell the driver where to go yet his words were inaudible.

We melded into the evening traffic, darkness falling over us in the backseat. His hand found my knee, warm and overbearing. My breathing sped up, hitched as his fingers moved between my legs. I clung to him, my knees falling apart giving his hand room to play. He cleared his throat loudly masking the groan that bellowed in his gut at the feel of my lace panties beneath his thick fingers.

He pushed the thin fabric to the side running a finger through my blatantly wet folds. I sunk my teeth into the meat of his arm smearing my lipstick across his exposed flesh. I gripped his wrist stilling his movements.

"No," I bit out in a whisper.

I couldn't—we couldn't. The space was too confined and I knew if he touched me the right way, I would blow the cover off of the naughty things we were doing in this poor man's taxi. I looked over catching the grin that stretched across his face. His hand abandoned me leaving me needy, exposed.

We reached the hotel in twenty minutes. He shifted into his jacket covering the traces of my lipstick. He paid the driver before climbing out. Turning, he held a hand out to help me to my feet. His hand pressed against the small of my back as we walked through the brightly lit lobby of the hotel.

On the outside we were composed but inside I was dying to feel him.

We barreled into the elevator occupying opposite sides not wanting to tease the other before we got to the room.

"You're trouble," he said running his gaze from my head down to my toes.

"Let's not forget who started it," I replied pushing my clutch underneath my arm as the elevator dinged to a stop.

He led the way out into the hallway pulling the hotel key from his back pocket. He stopped a few doors down pushing the key into the lock and pulling it out just as it turned green. We stepped into the shadows of the room groping our way inside. I kicked off my heels, ditched my purse and jacket in the floor. I was on him in one swift motion, every inch of our bodies hard pressed against one another.

He fisted his hands into my hair feeding me his groans as I fidgeted with the buckle of his pants. His hands gripped my backside crushing me to him, forcing me to feel what was hidden behind the jeaned barrier. Our feet moved stumbling over one another, crashing into walls as we scrabbled our way into the bathroom. He reached out flipping on the overhead light for the shower. Our breathing labored, our lips parted, and running dry. He yanked the shower door open extending behind me to turn on the water.

He stepped into the stream pressing my body against the cool tile. The sensation of the cold water turning warm rushed through me. He worked me out of my dress baring

4

my naked body to him. I clawed at his clothes with an erotic impatience. I had never needed a release so much in my life. He tightened his grip around my wrists pinning them to my sides.

"Slow down," he commanded. "We have all night."

He covered me with his overbearing presence. He reached up cupping my jaw in his hands, our lips inches apart. I swallowed hard, feeling as though I would combust if something didn't happen soon. He kissed me roughly, an underlying passion somewhere in there. His tongue found mine, deepening the kiss. I gripped his hips pulling him into me, trapping his erection between my thighs.

He reached down cupping the back of my legs, rearing me up off of my feet. My breath caught in my throat as he penetrated me fitting me almost perfectly. Our clothes lay at his feet tangled around his ankles. He didn't care anymore than I did. The sounds of our lovemaking echoed off of the shower walls.

He held me, worked me, kissed me, and made me feel as if what we were doing wasn't as forbidden of an act as people made it out to be. And in that moment, I fell in love with him all over again.

The sound of the room door opening and closing stirred me from my sleep. My eyes struggled to open. I felt overly exhausted from the heavy night of drinking. I rolled on my back letting the cool air dance across my nipples. Pushing up on my elbows, I drew the sheet up over my chest.

Tate Ellison hovered over the table draped in fresh white linen adorned with metal dome covered plates, pitchers of orange juice and water, and a lone rose that sat in an intricately decorated vase. He was shirtless dressed only in a pair of black lounge pants. The slight fabric gave way to the curve of his penis. My mouth twitched with the desire to taste him.

Tate was five years my senior, my English literature professor my first year of graduate school. I walked into class twenty minutes late after going to the wrong building and then getting lost in the right one. I practically tumbled down the steps of the lecture room the minute I saw him. He was over six feet tall with tanned skin and wavy dark brown hair. His lips pressed against his faultless white teeth in a smile, dimpled that reached up to his emerald green eyes.

His facial hair was well manicured and he was dressed laxly in a dark blue dress shirt rolled at the sleeves, the top two buttons undone showing a peek of the tattoo on his chest. He shoved his hands into his khaki pants and went back to teaching. Needless to say, I utilized every bit of his office hours after that. We flirted. He knew I wanted him yet every interaction was kept strictly professional.

Then, one day I couldn't take it anymore. I marched up to his office, barged in not giving a damn what he was doing, locked the door behind me and threw myself right into his lap. He fucked the hell out of me on his desk! Now, after five years, we were husband and wife.

"Good morning," I hummed sitting up fully.

He glanced over his shoulder at me. "Good morning, beautiful. Your mother called while you were sleeping."

I yawned stretching my arms widely letting the sheet fall away from me once more. His eyes trailed down to my protruding nipples. I laughed at his failure to be discreet.

"Did you answer it?"

"We're on vacation. What do you think?"

"No."

"Exactly."

I rubbed at the sore spot in my neck left behind from the way I'd slept just hours before. The chilled metal against my neck made me smile. I pushed my hand out to look at the ring that sat on my finger.

"You put it back on?" Tate inquired, as he popped a grape into his mouth before padding over to the bed.

"Role playing is cool but you're a married woman."

6

My eyes caught sight of his wedding band. "It was fun, wasn't it?"

He tilted forward planting a kiss on my lips. "You should have let me get you off in the back of the cab. That would have been the real fun."

"I didn't want to cause the man to crash."

Tate laughed fully. "You could have let go of your inhibitions for that one time. You would never see him again. Besides, it might have made his night."

He palmed my breast, squeezing my nipple in between his fingers.

"You could have gotten that poor boy killed in there last night from the way he was touching on you." I giggled pushing his hand away as I threw my legs over the edge of the bed.

I pulled the sheet with me, wrapping it around my torso before following behind him into the small dining area.

"It was merely acting. You think I was feeling that woman all in your face?"

"I didn't touch her though,"

"That's because I'm a lot crazier than you. How long have you been up?"

"Two hours maybe. I went down to the gym for a run on the treadmill."

"You're a beast. No wonder your stamina is through the roof."

"When your wife has a sexual appetite that is damn near insatiable, it has to be."

"You mean like now?" I teased.

He shook his head and chuckled. "You damn feign."

"You made me this way."

He caught me by the waist pulling me down into his lap. His fingers dug into my thighs pulling my legs apart to straddle him.

"Mr. Ellison, what happened to breakfast?" I panted.

He looked up at me, flashing that perfect smile that

always made me fall for him again and again.

"I think I want something a little bit sweeter."

A sound of pleasure stirred within me, that familiar friction subduing me. He lifted my chin with his finger, ran his warm tongue across my neck. My flesh began to heat, my core aching. He pulled the sheet from my body admiring me as if it was his first time seeing me in my rare form.

"Gosh, I love you Mrs. Ellison."

I ran my fingers through his hair tugging his head back gently to meet my eyes.

I whispered against his lips, "I love you more."

And it was then that we became lost in the moment.

Nenaya Renee - Romantic Author, Editor, and Self-Publisher

For Updates, Events, Exclusive Releases, And Much More,
Visit WWW.NENAYARENEE.COM and like her on Facebook!

Souls Intertwined
Because of the Storm

COMING SOON

Souls Unleashed

Get the exclusive download of "Loving Harper"
Now at, WWW.NENAYARENEE.COM

LOVE'S BATTLEFIELD
By Marie A. Norfleet

"McMillen and Associates law firm, Sarah McMillen, Assistant District Attorney speaking. How can I assist you, today?" Sarah impatiently answered her desk phone as she glanced at the clock on her office wall.

"Hello, beautiful" Sarah's face grew softer at the sound of Charlie's voice.

"Why hello there, handsome."

"We're still on for this weekend, right?" Charlie inquired.

"I wouldn't miss it for the world,"

"Great, I'll meet you up at the cabin around six. Are you sure you don't want me to just pick you up from the office and we'll leave from there?"

"No, I still have to run home and grab my bags. So, I'll meet you up there as planned." Sarah responded.

"Okay. Have it your way," Charlie chuckled. "I'll see you tonight."

"I can't wait." Sarah placed the phone's receiver into its cradle.

A slight tap on the office's wooden door, broke Sarah's train of thought.

"I hope I wasn't interrupting" Michael said in a seductive tone as he strolled over to Sarah's desk.

"Not, at all" Sarah allowed Michael to sit in her seat. She moaned as she straddled his lap and felt the bulge in his pants.

She began to place slow, subtle kisses along his neckline causing a slight shiver to travel down his spine. Though the feeling of her full lips felt good against his heated skin, Michael liked to be in control with everything he did, the bedroom or intimate sessions for that matter were of no exception. He lifted her and sat her on top of the desk, as he slowly removed her vaginally secreted underwear. Placing soft kisses on one thigh at time, he set one leg over each of his shoulders. Without warning or much effort, he stood up with all one hundred and sixty- five pounds of her busty frame on top of his shoulders.

With her arms wrapped securely around his neck, he gently placed her back against the cool wall and lowered to his knees. Her back arched as he skillfully used his tongue to part her moist folds. Quick animal-like laps of his tongue allowed him to savor her sweet dew. As he adjusted her legs on his shoulders, he was granted complete access to her hidden flower bud.

"Oh, Michael. Right there, baby!" Sarah shouted as she clawed at his freshly shaven head.

Michael continued his tongue torture as he got into a delectable sequence; lick, slurp, suck, blow, nibble. He knew she was nearing her peak by the way her body bucked uncontrollably against his face.

"Ah! Mi- Mi- Michael! I'm about to cu- ah! Sarah cried out in ecstasy as she rode the blissful orgasmic wave.

As her body trembled, he slipped on one of his, XL Magnum condoms. Without missing a beat, he lifted her off his shoulders and sat her on top of his engorged shaft. The shock of his entry sent her body into convulsions as she began to cream again from the gyrating of his hips. Leaning her back against the wall gave him leverage and support as he slowly thrust in and out of her carnal dwellings. A sweet melody of pleasurable moans, groans, and grunts filled the room as their bodies rhythmically clashed together.

"Ah! Go deeper, Michael! Go deeper, ba-by!" she howled.

He wanted to obey her commands but there was only one position that would allow him maximum penetration. "You want it deeper?" he thrust harder into her sensitive walls.

"Oh, yes! Give it to me" she yelled.

"You sure? That means I have to pull out," he whispered in her ear with repeated quick strokes.

"Oh, no. I don't want you to stop!" she hollered as she began to feel another orgasm building.

"No, you said you wanted it deeper so deeper is what you'll get" with that said, he pulled out abruptly. Michael chuckled slightly to himself as he watched her body slide down the wall. She closed her legs and gawked at him in awe.

"Get up, and bend that ass over on the desk" he demanded aggressively.

Without argument, she picked herself up on wobbly, unstable legs and assumed the position. He wasted no time as he plunged into her depths. Hissing loudly from a mixture of pain and pleasure, Sarah exhaled deeply. Taking her leg, he propped it up on the desk; leaving her treasure chest open for easy pickings. What were once slow and breath taking strokes became quick and deep, mind blowing pumps as he neared an orgasm of his own.

"Mmm. Ah! Throw it back for me, baby" He groaned as he pounded into her dripping wet box. On cue, she began throwing her ass back against his slippery thighs and the crashing of their bodies sounded like lightening ricocheting off a building.

"Oh shit, I am about to cum" he belted, as he felt the

tightening sensation in the pit of his abdomen.

"Me too!" she screamed.

He pounded her frame with quickened, profound strokes as they rode together into orgasmic harmony. Energetically spent and out of breath, he collapsed on her backside as the last few squirts of her womanly secretions ran down his thighs. No words were exchanged as he rose from the desktop and walked into the bathroom to clean up. Minutes later, he exited the bathroom and walked out of the office as if nothing out of the ordinary had transpired. Sarah took a few minutes to regroup and collect her thoughts before she went into her wardrobe to retrieve a fresh suit.

After refreshing herself and changing her clothes, she was out the door and heading downstairs to Michael's awaiting car.

Later on that night...

It was 7:30PM and the hollow whistle of the night's chilling air and the bustling of the freshly fallen fall leaves outside of the small cabin, caused spine tingling, chill bumps to raise all over Sarah's anemic body as she stared into the darkened wilderness.

"Charlie, did you figure out how to work that fireplace yet?" Sarah called out as she shook off an eerie cold chill.

"Just got it up and running, Hun" Charlie whispered as he passed her a mug of hot chocolate. He took her free hand and guided her over to the sofa in front of the fireplace.

"I am happy that you agreed to come up here with me this weekend. It feels good to have you to myself for a few days," He spoke as she laid her head back against his chest and placed a blanket over her shoulders.

"I am happy too," she smiled. "I was long overdue for a vacation."

"You and I, both" he responded with his signature wicked grin.

Without missing a beat, he placed his thin lips over hers. Their tongues intertwined with one another, dancing seductively. Charlie slowly pulled down the straps of Sarah's lace front bra until he was faced with a perfect set of 38 C's. He hungrily took her right nipple between his lips, lapping gently around the areola while pinching slightly on the left. A small moan escaped her lips.

Sarah's fingertips traced over his biceps and up his back as he used his tongue as a fiery guide to her hidden treasures. As he devoured her swollen bud, Sarah's back arched in ecstasy. Just as she was ready to release, the presence of a shadowy figure lurking in the window; startled her. Sarah slowly sat up and stared at the large glass window.

"What's wrong?" Charlie mumbled against her mound.

"I thought I saw someone or something standing in window" Sarah breathed nervously.

"Relax baby, there's no one around these neck of the woods for miles" he reassured her, as he began to place small kisses on her inner thigh.

A slight hiss escaped through her parted lips as she lay back against the cushions.

"Mmhm. Right there, baby" she moaned as she closed her eyes and rode his blue eyed face into a blissful orgasm.

The couple savored each other for hours, unaware of the envious eyes that watched from the large oak tree just a few yards away.

****

In bright red, 12:51AM displayed on the bedside alarm clock as Sarah turned over. Yawning and stretching out, expecting to feel Charlie's warm, broad chest; she was greeted with an empty bedside. Sleepily, Sarah swung her legs from the bed and placed her feet in her slippers before standing up and grabbing her robe from the headboard.

She shuffled down the hall to the restroom. Stopping at the doorway, she noticed the kitchen light on.

"Charlie?" she called out but got no response. Thinking nothing of it, she entered the bathroom and closed the door.

As she was getting up from the toilet, she caught a glimpse of herself in the mirror. Visible hickies trailed her neckline, she smiled as she reflected on the night's events. Turning on the shower, she climbed in the stall and allowed the steaming hot water to massage her aching body.

Fifteen minutes later, a soft rapid knock on the door interrupted her train of thought.

"Come in, Charlie. You should come join me, the water feels great" she yelled over the shower water. A cool breeze blew through the curtain as she heard the door open. But, when he didn't enter; she turned off the shower.

"Charlie?" she called out as she peeked outside of the curtain. Stepping out of the stall, a smile spread across her face when she read "follow me" on a small card that lay on the floor. Walking out into the hall, a trail of rose petals led her to the basement door.

She followed the petals into the basement and down the wooden stairs. When she reached the bottom step, a blindfold was placed over her eyes. Amused by his efforts, she decided to play along. She held his hand as he guided her through the darkness. When they stopped, she began to take off the blindfold.

"Don't," she heard him whisper from a small distance ahead of her. "Use your legs to feel for the bed in front of you." She did as he instructed.

"Take off your robe and lay down" he commanded.

When she laid down, she was met by the coolness of silk sheets.

Her heart began to race and her breathing picked up anxiously as she felt his hands roam her body. Grabbing her hands above her head, he roughly tied each arm to its own bed post. Excitement filled her, as she felt his body lift from hers. The coolness, from a string of pearls being rubbed over her belly; caused her to shiver. She shrieked in ecstasy as the pearls were slowly inserted into her and gently pulled out.

The enclosing smell of Charlie's cologne and Irish spring soap, made her arm hair rise as the soft tip of his man pole brushed against her lips. She stuck out her tongue and teased him with short, circular motions around the rim. She caught her breath as the feeling of his untamed hair brushed against her abdomen. Without warning, Charlie rose from the bed. Anxiously, she awaited his next touch and exhaled slowly when she felt the bed lower on her left side.

A sharp excruciating pain replaced the sensual feeling soon after. The sharp object was lifted and plunged into her stomach again, with more force than the first time. She screamed as she blacked out from the pain. She came to, what felt like hours later and couldn't hold back the vomit. Wide eyed, lifeless and covered in blood; lay Charlie and his severed penis.

"Charlie! Oh, Charlie" she cried. She glanced around the dimly lit room frantically. A hooded figure began to emerge from a corner.

She struggled to get free from her restraints as she pleaded for her life. "I don't know what you are after but if its money, I have plenty of it. Please don't kill me and I will make you rich beyond your wildest dreams."

The sounds of sniffling surprised her.

"All I ever wanted was, you" the figure responded as it neared the bed. Slowly, the assailant pulled off its hood.

The tears began to flow uncontrollably from Sarah's eyes as she stared back into the cold eyes of her life long best friend, Michelle also known as Michael.

"Michelle? What are you doing here?" she whimpered.

"I could ask you the same Sarah, but that answer I already know," Michelle sat on the edge of the bed, twiddling the blood stained knife in her hand.

"What I don't know, is why? Why would you do this Sarah? Was I not enough for you?"

"O-of course you were, Michelle" Sarah stammered.

"So what was it? What made you stray and destroy fifteen years of marriage?" A male's voice spoke out from the darkened corner.

"Oh my god, Trevor help me! She's crazy! Baby, please!" Sarah pleaded with her husband.

Trevor let out a wicked laugh as he stood beside Michelle.

"She's the one having not one but two affairs, and you're the crazy one" Trevor chuckled, Michelle joined in.

"I gave up everything for you, Sarah. Worked two jobs just to put you through law school, took care of our daughter before and after she got ill, stuck by your side during the grieving process over the loss of her and this is how you repay me?" Trevor screamed.

"You couldn't be happy with having your cake and eating it, you just had to bake the motherfucker too. See, this is what happens when you get too greedy Sarah. You don't get to play with people's feelings, lives and emotions. Every action in life has a reaction, and these are the repercussions behind your choices." Michelle stood from the bed, stripped of her robe and pushed Trevor down into a chair that sat beside the bed.

Slowly straddling him reverse cowgirl style, Michelle moved her body upward, teasing Trevor with threatening penetration while staring into the eyes of Sarah.

"How do you like that, Sarah?" Michelle hissed.

"Fuck you!" Sarah spat as blood spilled from her lips.

"I guess she doesn't like that," Michelle chuckled.

"Sarah, it was me who provided you the shoulder to cry on those nights when you thought he was out cheating on you," Michelle rotated her hips quickly, as she felt Trevor tugging on her to sit on his bulging member.

"Me, who drove you back and forth to your secret counseling sessions because you didn't want him to know how messed up in the head you really were. It was me, who helped you piece your life back together after your father stole your innocence and turned you into the nymphomaniac that you are." Trevor's movements ceased upon hearing of his wife's childhood abuse.

"Say what? Why didn't you ever tell me about your father?" Trevor questioned Sarah as he tried to lift Michelle off of him.

"She didn't tell you because she didn't need to tell you. Truth is, she never really wanted to be with you, Trevor. You were just the fool who went in unprotected and knocked her up. Marrying you, seemed like the right thing to do but she was never in love with you. Her heart has always belonged to me and if you hadn't interfered when you did, we would've been happy!" Michelle screamed as she skillfully removed a small razor blade from her mouth.

Swiftly, she turned her body around so that she was sitting face to face with him.

"Now, you'll never interfere with our love again" Michelle expertly moved the blade from one end of Trevor's throat to the other.

"Trevor!" Sarah weakly screamed. Trevor clasped his hands over his gushing neck.

Michelle rose from his lap, smiling at her work.

"I begged you to get rid of him and you were too weak to do so. Now, look what you've made me do. I loved you, Sarah! Why couldn't you see that? I have dedicated my life to you, since we were twelve! Why couldn't you love me the same?" Michelle cried as she pushed Charlie's body onto hardwood floor and climbed onto the bed.

"I did love you, Michelle. It may not have been how you wanted me to but I did love you. I just wanted more than you could give. I wanted children, you couldn't give me that. I eventually wanted a husband, you could never be that. I needed the comforts of warm and embracing arms that made me feel protected." Sarah took a second to contemplate her next words, knowing they'd be her last; she wanted them to be truthful.

"Yes, I felt safe whenever I was with you. But, there is a certain security that only a man can provide to a woman and you could never give me that because you are not a man. No matter how low you kept your haircut, how flat you kept your breast taped, how many days you spent in the gym; you could never be the man that I needed. And, I know that I didn't treat Trevor right all the time but he was that man. He was my husband and you were my friend, I thought you understood that.

I never knew you wanted to be more than that. I mean, I guess there were some signs but I was too selfish to pay attention. For that, I am sorry. I am sorry I never considered your feelings, I am sorry that I wasn't there the way you wanted me to be and I am sorry that I was not the woman you craved for me to be." Sarah let it all pour out. Yes, she loved Michelle but never enough in that manner, to spend her life with her.

"I could've been all you that desired, provided you with all that you wanted; if only you'd have given me the chance Sarah. But, it's too late for that now. Now, we'll never know what could've been."

Michelle plunged the knife deep into her own torso, twice. She lay beside Sarah as she bled out, and stared into her eyes as she faded into the darkness. Silent tears fell from Sarah's eyes as she watched the woman who once meant the world to her, take her last breath. Sarah couldn't believe that everything she'd treasured most in life; she'd lost it all within moments. And all for what? A few blissful encounters with her best friend, a couple of out of town trips with her lover, a lifetime of lies, regrets, shame and some really treasured memories with her husband?

Weakly taking a deep breath, Sarah let the tears flow from her eyes like rivers as she freely succumbed to her own wounds.

COMING SOON FROM
MARIE "THE GAME CHANGER" NORFLEET

Domino Effect
Domino Effect 2: Picking Up The Pieces
Her Husband, Is My Man
Costly Decisions (Book 2 of the "Costly Decisions" Series)
Remembering Our Vows (Book 3 of "CD" Series)
Love's Prisoner
Little Orphan Angie: Falling Victim To The Game
Domino Effect 3: The Last Of A Dying Breed

I am also the CEO of Game Changing Publications, where we are currently accepting submissions in the following genres: Urban Fiction, Street Lit, Chick Lit, Drama, Suspense, Erotica, Romance, Mystery and Young Adult All submissions can be submitted to submissions@gamechangingpublications.com for consideration.

<u>Game Changing Publications offers the following services:</u>
Copy Editing
Developmental Editing
E-Book Conversion
Formatting
Typesetting
Graphic Design (bookmarks, fliers, business cards, etc)
Printing Services (bookmarks, fliers, business cards, etc)
Proof Reading
Synopsis Writing (all genres)
Test Reading (Includes review on Amazon, B&N, etc)
Typing Services
Web Design

Turnaround time is typically two-three weeks, depending
on services contracted.
For all inquiries, please email:
Services@gamechangingpublications.com

Follow me on the following sites, for the latest updates:
Facebook:
https://www.facebook.com/TheGameChangersLounge/?fre
f=ts
Twitter: https://twitter.com/authormarien
Instagram: https://www.instagram.com/theauthoressmarien/

And, check out my websites:
www.gamechangingpublications.com
www.MarieANorfleet.com

LESSON LEARNED
By Sapphire James

Hailey and I attended Bellaire High School in Houston, TX near Meyerland Mall. My name is Lake and I pretty much kept to myself. Well, until I met Hailey. She moved into the same apartment complex I lived in and we hit it off instantly. She was the total opposite of me. I was timid and didn't like attention. She was outgoing and made her presence known whenever she entered a room. She and I were smarter than most of the kids in our area. Therefore, we had to be bused to a fancy school because we were both part of the magnet program.

I'd never really paid much attention to any of the boys at our school, but I had the biggest crush on a chocolate cutie named Kelvin Johnston. He was gorgeous. Every time the bus pulled up to his stop I would become anxious. Butterflies didn't explain the feeling I had in the pit of my stomach whenever he was around. With a slight puddle between my legs and my heart about to jump out my chest, this was the norm for me. Kelvin gave me this feeling twice a day and he had no clue.

"Bitch, whatchu wearing to the concert Saturday? Do you need to borrow something out of my closet?" Hailey rambled. "Hello? Heffa, do you hear me talking to you?"

I'd heard bits and pieces of what Hailey was saying, but I was more focused on the bulge in Kelvin's jeans. Secretly, I wondered what it looked like, what it felt like…shit, what it tasted like. I had never seen a penis up close, but I could just imagine. I never had the desire until Kelvin's fine ass hit the scene.

"Umm, what?" I uttered. "Yeah, yeah, the concert. Right, I don't know what I'm wearing."

"Bitch, when are you gonna stop acting all shy and tell that dude how you feel? A'ight, you gon' mess around and somebody's gonna snatch him right from under your ass." Hailey nudged me.

"Whatever," I popped my lips. "I ain't playing. I am shy. What if he doesn't like me? Lawd, my heart couldn't take it."

"Girl stop! As fine as you are? You know damn well there are so many dudes tryna get at you it ain't even funny. Hell, why would he not like you with all of that ass? Tell you what, how about if I talk to him for you? You know…feel him out a little bit."

My eyes widened at the thought, "You would do that for me?"

"Of course. You're my bestie and I want you to be happy. I'll do it today during lunch, but after that it is all on you honey."

For the remainder of the day I was on pins and needles. Hailey and I had P.E together, but there was no time to discuss anything because of all days, Mrs. Kotton decided to work us like Hebrew slaves. I wouldn't see her again until we got on the bus and I was pissed. I wanted to know what she said and what Kelvin's reaction was. Hell, I was worse than a child on Christmas day waiting for her parents to wake up so she could open her gifts.

The day dragged on until finally the bell rang and it was time to go home. As soon as I heard the first chime I was out of there. I didn't even wait for my teacher to dismiss us. I didn't have time for that shit. I was on a mission.

Luckily, I made it to the bus before Hailey and Kelvin. Looking out of the window I felt a little twinge as I watched the two of them approach the bus while laughing.

"What the hell are they laughing at?" I thought.

Kelvin allowed Hailey to get on the bus first as she took her usual seat beside me. He opted to sit directly in front of us. Before I could ask her about their conversation, Kelvin had already turned around to face me.

"Hey Lake," He winked. "Here's my number. Call me tonight. I can't wait to talk to you."

Kelvin had braces and that made him look even sexier to me. I wasn't prepared for him to be so forward, so I didn't know how to respond to him.

I swallowed the huge lump in my throat as I replied, "Okay."

Yep, that was all I could say at the moment. Kelvin Johnston had given me his home phone number and couldn't wait for me to call him. I was on cloud nine. There was just one problem. My parents were so damn strict and I had to be off of the phone by nine o'clock and I wasn't really allowed to talk to boys. Well, I could but my nosey ass mama would sneak on the phone to see if I was talking about sex, so I decided it wasn't worth it.

Mama had a bad habit of embarrassing me when she picked up the phone to notify me it was past my curfew. I hated when she did that shit!

"Hailey," I whispered. "You know I can't talk to boys on the phone. How am I going to get around that?"

"Oh don't worry," She assured me. "I have that all covered. I'ma call you on three-way so your mom's won't suspect a thing. That way you can talk to your boo without her snooping and shit."

Yep, that is why I fucked with Hailey. She was a pro at finding ways to do dirt. If there was a loophole to be found, her ass would be the one to figure it out.

"Okay cool."

Kelvin and I had been dating for almost four months and I couldn't have been happier. Our nightly routine went undetected. Every night Hailey would call me around seven o'clock, merging Kelvin in the call. We had two hours to talk about everything under the sun until my mama would pick up the phone telling me to say good night to my lil friend. I knew my mama meant well, but she made me want to pull my damn eye lashes out.

I felt like the luckiest girl in the world to be on the arms of Kelvin Johnston. All the girls at Bellaire thought he was fine, but he was quiet and kept to himself. That's probably why I liked him. He reminded me of myself. Every morning Kelvin and I would manage to slip away from Hailey to steal a few kisses. I could honestly say I loved that dude. I think it was love at first sight for me. Thoughts of him consumed me daily.

One day after we'd slipped away, I noticed Hailey had an attitude. This was so unlike her and I was about to put her ass in her place. I knew damn well she couldn't be jealous as many times as her ass had disappeared on me to be with a nigga. She had me so fucked up.

"Where the hell y'all been?" She demanded.

"Bitch, why you acting all salty? We were underneath the bleachers. Why?!" I frowned.

Hailey glared at Kelvin with her arms crossed. I was confused and on the brink of molly-whopping her ass. However, nothing could have prepared me for what followed.

"Did you tell her, Kelvin?"

"Tell me what?" I clenched my teeth.

"I'm sorry," He apologized.

I didn't know what the hell was going on, but I began to tremble and my stomach went from feeling beautiful butterflies to having knots.

"What are you sorry for Kelvin? I asked.

"Look," Hailey sucked her teeth. "It's like this, Kelvin and I talk every day. You have a nine o'clock curfew. So when you get off the phone, we keep talking. We've discovered that we have a lot in common and we are in love. We've been together for three months now. It was never our intention to hurt you, but it just happened. Also, I'm pregnant."

I couldn't believe what I was hearing. My ears had to be deceiving me. If this was a joke, it was a terrible one. Did that bitch say they were in love? Better yet, did she say she was pregnant? Wow! It all made sense. Every time I made a move to kiss him that day, Kelvin would playfully back away from me. I felt sick to my stomach.

"How could they do this shit to me?" I thought.

My mama was right about her hoe-ass. I thought my mama just didn't like her because to be honest, she didn't like anyone. But this time she was right on the money. This was a huge blow to my heart. The one person I thought I could trust had betrayed me in the most unforgiveable way. She knew how I felt about him. What was I supposed to say? Nothing. I felt warm tears forming around the rims of my eyes, so I turned to walk away. I'd be damned if I let those two bitches see me shed one damn tear.

For the next two months that situation was the talk of the school. I heard every whisper and felt every stare. I could read the minds of my peers. It hurt so badly to endure such a heartache while it was being displayed right before my eyes. Hailey had turned evil. Actually, I always knew she had certain tendencies. She could be sweet when she wanted to be, and downright demonic when she felt the need. If she wanted something or someone, she would not stop until she got it. I just never thought I would be on the receiving end of her dagger.

As the weeks passed I swear I could see Hailey's little baby bump. We still had seventh period physical education together and it pained me too badly to see her pregnant by the boy I'd loved since middle school. I felt my stomach churn as it warned me my lunch was on its way back up. I quickly excused myself to bathroom. I made it just in time to throw up and wipe mouth. Moments later I heard two voices.

"Reagan girl, I can't believe his dumb ass fell for the okey doke! I always knew he was simple. I mean, how could he think these babies are his? Girl, by the time we did it I was already six weeks. Idiot." She laughed.

"Humph, what the hell you gon do when you have those babies early and they look nothing like him?" Reagan questioned.

Oh my God! This hoe was pregnant with twins and they weren't even Kelvin's! I felt my blood boil as I continued to listen to the conversation.

"I ain't gon tell him shit! They can be premature and I will just tell him they look me. Problem solved. Besides, he just wants to be a good daddy to his babies. I got it made. Even his parents are excited and have bought all kinds of shit for the babies and for me. By the time he figures out the babies aren't his they'll be eighteen."

"Hailey you better be careful," Reagan warned. "You know this shit can blow up in your face and if it does it's going to be a big ass mess."

"Don't you worry about me," She swooped her braids behind her ear. "I got this. This ain't my first go around pulling a stunt like this."

"Did you ever tell Keon you were pregnant?"

"Hell naw, I don't need his broke ass fucking my plans up. He doesn't have shit to offer my babies. I needed to make sure all three of us will be taken care of and that is exactly what I am doing. And you better not let me find out you said anything to anyone because you are the only person that knows Kelvin ain't the daddy. Don't make me have to beat the shit out of you. Okay?" Hailey countered.

I wanted to fly my ass out of that bathroom stall and dropkick the shit out of her. She didn't even want Kelvin. She just did this because Kelvin's family had money, so he was the better choice. How could I have been so blind? Just as they were about to leave the bathroom I dry heaved again and prayed they didn't hear me. I waited for five minutes to make sure they were gone. To my surprise, Hailey was waiting for me when I walked out of the stall.

"Tuh, of course it would be you to over hear everything. Okay, so you know my secret. Now what?"

"I don't have shit to say about it. You're a scandalous bitch and if you weren't pregnant I'd monkey-stomp yo' ass." I threatened.

"Yeah well, I am pregnant. And even if I weren't, you still ain't bout that life. So bye bitch," She waved her hand. "Oh, if you do decide to open ya mouth, you gon have to see me."

The funny thing was, she had just told on herself. Kelvin's step-sister Kelly walked in just as Hailey finishing her sentence.

"Bitch, you mean my brother ain't those babies' daddy? That's right, I heard everything you and Reagan said. You been using him all of this time? Oh, you know I'm bout to tell him right fucking now. This shit is over!" Kelly yelled.

Kelly sprinted out of the bathroom in such a haste, she didn't even ask if she could leave class. She just rushed to Kelvin's English class and immediately pulled him out of class. Hailey trailed after her and since I desperately wanted to see the bomb drop, I followed behind the both of them. I didn't give a damn about getting in trouble, this would be worth the detention I would receive.

I watched as Kelly informed Kelvin of what had been going on behind his back while Hailey attempted to plead her case. It was the craziest shit I'd ever seen. Karma really was a bitch. Kelvin was so livid he ran down the stairs as Hailey followed behind. However, things took a turn for the worst as she missed a step and went flailing down the stairs. Immediately blood was everywhere. I didn't have time to think about the pain Hailey had caused me.

I ran to her side to help her in any way I could, but I couldn't stop the bleeding. The ambulance got there and later that night I had gotten word that Hailey had indeed lost her babies. Part of me should have felt vindicated, but I actually felt bad for her. The next day Kelvin asked if he could have a moment of my time when we got off the bus.

"Lake, I am so sorry for how things transpired. I never meant to hurt you. You have to believe that." He apologized.

"Kelvin, how am I supposed to believe what you are saying to me right now? We dated four months and three of those you were screwing my best friend. I had already told you how I felt about you. You were my first love and you hurt me the very first chance you got." I reminded him.

Kelvin allowed his head to fall to his chest with embarrassment. I could tell he was sorry, but what was I supposed to do? Okay, so he was sorry. Was I supposed to just forgive and forget like the shit hadn't damn near destroyed me? Was he sorry because he hurt me, or was he sorry because he found the babies weren't his and he had been played too? I was so fucking confused.

"Lake, it was so much more to it," He began to explain. "From the very first time we spoke on the phone Hailey came at me. She put so much on it. She was telling me everything she would let me do to her. Some of the things she mentioned I'd never even heard of. I knew she was easy. So, I made a terrible choice, but I am truly sorry Lake."

"Okay, so because Hailey's hoe-ass basically handed you the pussy on a platter you had to be a typical nigga and indulge? I never would have thought that about you, but I see you are just like the rest of these dog-ass niggas. It's all good Kelvin. I'm glad we had this little talk because now I see what kind of person you truly are. Bye!"

"Lake, I'm trying to tell you that I'm fucking sorry!" He yelled.

"I heard you!" I yelled back as I continued to walk away.

I hadn't cried in over a month. After a few weeks I'd decided this situation was no longer worth my tears. However, there was so much strife going on in my life it was unavoidable. As I made my way to the bathroom, my tears stung my eyes. I thought I would feel better about Kelvin apologizing to me, but that wasn't the case; I actually felt worse. How could that be? Why did this dude have my heart so tangled?

The rest of the year passed by swiftly. Before I realized it, prom and graduation had taken place and I was preparing to go away to college. I had been accepted into Texas A&M University in College Station. I was enthusiastic about leaving home for the ultimate college experience. I'd worked hard over the last few months to put my pain and heartache behind to be included in the bucket of shit from my past. Especially, all of the shit with Hailey and Kelvin. I was stepping into my adult life.

I had been at Texas A&M for a year and had settled in quite nicely. My roommate was the best roommate I could ask for. I'd made a few friends that I genuinely knew had my back. All was well at school until one night I saw a ghost from my past. Walking into Evans Library my heart stopped as a familiar vision of loveliness made his way to me.

"Hi Lake! Muah!" Kelvin greeted as he hugged and kissed me.

"Umm, hey," I mumbled. "What are you doing here?"

Instantly, an all too recognizable longing between my thighs reminded me of why I fell in love with him in the past. Kelvin was the only man to ever have this effect on my mind, body and soul. I thought these feelings faded away because he was out of sight and out of mind, but I was terribly wrong. I wondered if he could tell how wet I was just from him saying hi to me?

"I just enrolled," he answered. "Never mind that. Whatchu about to do right now?"

"Nothing," I lied. "I mean, I was about to check out a book but it can wait. Why?" Lord Jesus, forgive me for what I was thinking and for the sinning I knew was about to take place. I said to myself.

"Okay cool. Come with me." He smiled as he grabbed my hand.

In less than fifteen minutes, we arrived at Kelvin's townhouse. Of course, he lived off campus and it was very nice. His taste was very contemporary furnished in black and red. Our high school colors for Bellaire were red and white. I'm sure that had something to do with his décor.

I continued to admire his townhouse as he fled upstairs for a brief moment. I couldn't help but wonder what the hell he was doing up there. Suddenly, he appeared downstairs.

"Here this is for you," He handed me a medium sized box. "I'd planned on giving this to you after graduation, but you left so damn fast. So, I just held onto it. I've been praying I would bump into you, but I just didn't know how that would happen and then there you were."

"Kelvin...I don't know what to say. This is so..." I began to cry before I could finish my sentence. In that moment all of my emotions escaped me. "Why now?"

Kelvin pulled me into him as he rested his forehead on mine, "I promised myself that if you ever gave me the chance I would live the rest of my life trying to make up for the pain I had caused you. So will you allow me to do that?"

As I listened to Kelvin's sincere soliloquy, I forgave him wholeheartedly. Maybe I was stupid for still wanting this man after the pain and embarrassment he put me through, but my heart was in charge of what I wanted and needed at the moment. There was something indifferent about him and I wanted to get to know the new Kelvin.

"Are you going to open your gift Lake?"

"Oh, yeah," I answered as I ripped the box open. "Oh my God! Kelvin it's beautiful!"

Inside of the box was a scrap book of every letter we had written each other, accompanied with pictures he had printed of us. There was also a Tiffany bracelet with a heart charm with the words "Forever Sorry" engraved on the back of it.

"I'm so glad you like it."

"I love it," I smiled. "In fact, I still love you!"

We gazed into each other's eyes as the heat between us continued to rise. I placed my arms around his neck as I stood on my toes to kiss him. We were long overdue for this kiss and for what was to follow. I wanted to feel him. I had always wanted to feel him in the worst way. His manhood rubbed against my stomach just the way I remembered it when we used to go underneath the bleachers.

Kelvin knew what I wanted and he was all too obliging to give it to me. He filled my mouth with his tongue and placed his hands under my shirt to fondle my perky breast. The feeling was divine, but that is not where I wanted his hands to touch me. I grabbed his hand and slowly guided him down to my creamy center. He caught on fast as he inserted three thick fingers in a slow rhythm bringing me to the point of an earth shaking orgasm. My breathing was choppy and beads of sweat fell from my brow as my body fell into him.

"Damn Lake, your name describes you perfectly baby," he teased. "I want more, but I wanna do this right. We've both waited too long. I'ma make love to you, not fuck you. C'mon, we're going upstairs."

Before I could answer him, Kelvin had scooped me into

his arms and carried me upstairs to his bedroom where Jasmine scented candles were lit and soft music was playing. The ambiance was perfect for making love and my body was trembling with anxiety. Kelvin removed my shirt, and helped me step out of my sweat pants. His strong hands traveled up and down my thighs as he licked his lips. He pulled my black lace panties down to my ankle so he could help me step out of them.

"Mmm," He sniffed. "I'm keeping these."

I didn't respond. I couldn't respond. I stood there allowing the air to kiss my skin while he admired my body. He picked me up again this time placing me in the center of his king sized bed. Kelvin was in tune with me. He kept his eyes on me with every feather-like touch.

Foreplay was Kelvin's forte and I welcomed that, but I wanted him to fill me up with that dick. While in deep thought, I felt his tongue attack apex of my thighs. His taste buds were warm and hungry for my nectar. Uncontrollably, I gave him what he thirsted for. Finally, he gave me what I had been yearning for. My legs shuddered as he invaded my soul, playing with every fantasy I'd ever had of him.

His rod was long and thick. He hit every wall there was to hit. Once again, being in tune with my body, his thrusts matched my breathing pattern. He leveled himself over me as he stared into my eyes. Kelvin was a very attentive lover. I was losing my mind with every orgasm.

"Oh my God Kelvin!" I screamed. "You feel so fucking good! I love this dick!"

"Mmm Lake," Kelvin whispered. "This is the best pussy I've ever had. Cum for me baby. Cum for daddy."

On que, I soaked him with my love and created a huge wet spot in the middle of his bed. I could tell he was not too far behind me. His pace increased and his breathing became labored.

"Damn Lake!" He moaned. "Fuuuh, there it is. You feel it? You feel that hot nut coating your walls? Ssss…ahhh!"

After that day we spent together, Kelvin and I were inseparable. We ended up moving in together after graduating from Texas A&M and eventually got married. Kelvin kept his word, he spent the rest of his life loving me and treating me like a queen. After being married for six years, we were finally welcoming our first child together.

"You ready babe?" Kelvin asked.

"Yes sir," I breathed through my contractions. "Let's meet this lil baby doll we've been waiting on for the last nine months."

"I can't wait," He admitted. "I hope she looks just like you with long, curly hair and big brown eyes." Two hours later, River Kaleena Johnston, was born on September 9, 2012.

Our lives were perfect and I am glad that I decided to give love another chance. Kelvin was a successful engineer and I was an English teacher. For a long time, my mother did not approve of Kelvin after he'd hurt me in the past but that was an early lesson for me. Never have a female around you and your man. Some shit your friends don't need to be a part of.

AVAILABLE ON AMAZON

His Work Wife
Cumming of Age

Second installments to both books coming soon!

Reach out to Author Sapphire James:
Email: mssapphirej@gmail.com
Twitter: @mssapphirejay
Facebook: www.facebook/daphne.garrett1

IT START WITH A LIKE
By M. Dawn

They had been talking on the phone on and off for the last four weeks. Ever since he liked a post she wrote on her friend Sandra's Facebook page. Not only was Sandra a mutual friend but Sameer and Keri had a lot of things in common; favorite authors, movies and singers. They wanted to visit some of the same places and both of them took their relationship with God very seriously.

Since accepting Christ as their personal Savior, there had been some slip-ups on each side but after Sameer nearly lost his life, being shot by the husband of a woman who he was dealing with and Keri almost dying from an ectopic pregnancy, they each decided that they would rededicate themselves and wait on the Lord to bless them with their mate.

Neither had any idea that a like on a post would lead to inbox messages, then emails in the morning and evening, to all throughout the day text messages that led to phone calls. Phone calls that would last two to three hours. Phone calls that ended with "You hang up" "No, you hang up." "OK, on the count of three, we both hang up." Phone calls that revealed dark secrets, silly jokes and debates on healthcare, the state of black youth and what they each saw for their future.

Sameer was just about everything that Keri wanted in a mate; he fit just about everything her pastor taught the single women at her church that a man should be and have, if he was serious about you as a woman and a potential wife.

Pastor Pat said during a breakfast with the single women that there was to be no missionary dating; if he didn't have a relationship with the Lord or wasn't saved, you couldn't date him, thinking he would get saved. There were too many men faking it just to get close to a woman and pounce when she was vulnerable because she let her guard down, due to being swayed by the pretty words.

Check number one for Sameer: he was invested in his relationship with God, serving as the assistant youth pastor at his parents' ministry. Check number two: he had his own car, a brown 2012 brown Lexus. Pastor Pat went on to tell her spiritual daughters that he also must have his own home, he must have a job, know how to spend money wisely and that the young lady should pay attention how he respected his parents, especially his mother.

With Sameer, there were checks all across the board. He lived in the two-story, five-bedroom house that his maternal grandparents had built for him upon earning his Bachelor's degree in the field of Criminology. Sameer was a police officer with the Henrico County Police Department, on his way to being promoted to Detective, after passing the test with flying colors.

With the stocks and bonds that his paternal grandparents brought for Sameer each year since turning thirteen, he was sitting on pretty beautiful nest egg, splurging only in a few of his weaknesses; clothes, books and art. As far as loving and respecting his parents, that was a given. The youngest of three boys, Sameer saw the good, the bad and even the sometimes ugly in his parents' marriage; especially in the beginning stages of what is now a successful, community based ministry located in the Highland Springs area of Virginia, that his parents started thirteen years ago.

Sameer saw his mother stand by her husband, supporting him in prayer and often times denying herself vacations, dates and even romantic nights at home with her husband as he was often called away to counsel and financially support church members or travel with his overseer as his chief adjutant, while maintaining a full time job because it wasn't easy raising three boys. Sameer's mother often took a job here or there to make sure that her household did not falter, even with Sameer's father adamant about his wife staying home and seeing after the family.

In his conversation with Keri, he was glad to see that she possessed a lot of his mother's qualities and a few of her characteristics. Keri was on her way to getting her degree in Early Childhood Education and had a clear business plan already in place. It was her goal to own and operate a Youth and Family Development Center, focused on providing services essential to those in the lower levels of income.

She lived with her grandparents since the age of twelve, after losing her parents in a hit and run accident while on their way to catch a flight to a church convention; that her mother was to be one of the keynote speakers. Because of the quarter of a million-dollar life insurance policy that Keri's father took out when Keri was five, allowed her to be in a position to never work a day in her life. But, like the example set by her grandfather and several aunts and uncles, Keri could not see herself squander the blessing that the Lord provided her.

Through watching the over fifty years of marriage and forty-five years of parenting through her grandparents, Silas and Carri Ann Pack, Keri had wonderful examples of what she desired and expected out of the right kind of marriage with the right kind of man as her mate.

Keri often bragged to Sameer that she could cook from scratch just about anything and never took short cuts when he asked her one day about baking.

"There has never been a box mix of any type cross my Nana's threshold," Keri told him. "My grandmother would likely have a fit! Nana always said Keri, a wise woman takes care of her household, while standing side by side on many of days as they cooked, baked, sewed and or cleaned."

Now the day finally arrived. The day that they would finally see each other, face to face. Yeah, there had been the liking of selfies posted on Facebook and pictures attached to Sunday morning texts; but those were only images. Today, he would see just how brown Keri's eyes were. Just where she would fit against his chest as he hugged her and how the Organza by Givenchy smelled against her skin, a fragrance recommended by his sister-in-law Elicia, which he sent her as a birthday present earlier in the month.

Dressed in a pair of True Religion jeans and a gray V neck cashmere sweater, Sameer slid his feet into his black Kenneth Coles loafers, picked up his wallet, car keys and IPhone off the dresser and made his way downstairs to get his black motor cycle jacket. After asking Keri out a couple of times, she finally said Yes.

Saying Yes to going out on a date, which would allow them to interact with one another to see if they really had chemistry. Her only stipulation was that it be to a place that would allow conversation but not compromise their witness or integrity. That was one thing that Sameer really liked about Keri; she never wanted people to look at him any other way. She wanted them to see him as the man of God and the community minded man that he was.

Programming her address into the GPS, Sameer got on

I95 and made his way to Keri's residence twenty minutes away in Chesterfield, VA. His radio tuned to Praise 104.7, Bryan Courtney Wilson's "Worth Fighting For" began to play as Sameer paid the toll and made his way across I895. About 10 minutes later, the GPS voice informed Sameer that his destination was located just ahead on the right.

Parking behind a red 2014 Nissan Murano with plates that read KDZ 1ST, Sameer got out, walked up the pathway and rang the doorbell. A tall gray haired man who had eyes just like Keri's answered the door.

"Hello, Sameer. Keri's expecting you. My name is Silas Pack, I'm Keri's grandfather. Come on in" Grandpa Silas said, reaching out and shaking the young man's hand. After shaking hands, they walked through the foyer until they approached the entrance to the family room.

Sitting on the couch was Keri and her grandmother, Nana Carrie. They were looking at an episode of Braxton Family Values, where Bishop T. D. Jakes was counseling the family on a beautiful sixty-inch flat screen TV. The TV was mounted on the wall, connected to the centerpiece of a black entertainment center that housed DVD's, a IPod deck and various family photos in decorative frames.

Looking up, Keri smiled and arose from the couch to greet Sameer, with a little too much pep in her step for Nana Carrie.

"Slow down, young lady," Nana Carrie said smiling. "Your young man is not going anywhere. Are you, young man?"

Sameer shook his head and said, "No ma'am" bypassing Keri, and reintroducing himself to Nana Carrie. With the scent of jasmine filling his nostrils, Sameer said, "Good afternoon Nana Carrie, if I may call you that. Keri has talked so much about you and Papa Si, I feel like I have known you all of my life."

With a slight chuckle, Nana Carrie responded.

"That's fine, Sameer, is it? The names you young folk

have nowadays." Laughing, Nana Carrie looked up at her husband. "Whatever happened to James, Charles, Robert? Good, strong names. Names that opened doors."

"Now Luvie," Grandpa Silas spoke. "There is nothing wrong with this young man's name. From what Baby Girl tells us, his name did not hold him back from the many accomplishments he has made for one so young."

Twisting up her lips and about to debate her husband's response, Nana Carrie thought twice after noticing the stern look that Grandpa Silas gave her. Looking at Keri and grinning, Sameer walked up to her and said "Hello."

Smiling, Keri returned the greeting and inquired, "Did you have any trouble getting here?"

"No," he replied with a smile. "With the GPS and Siri – Easy as 1,2,3."

In person, Sameer had to admit to himself that Keri was even more beautiful. Dressed in a beige cowl necked sweater with shades of gold, fuchsia and blue which made up an abstract design, a pair of Seven for All Mankind skinny jeans and brown calf skin boots with wedge heels. Keri stood at a height of 5'6". Her brown hair, with blonde highlights was pulled off her face in tight curls. She had a fuchsia flower pinned on the left. And, she was wearing the perfume; it smelled wonderful on her. He was going to have to really thank his sister-in-law for the recommendation.

"Would you like something to drink, Sameer? Nana Carrie and I just baked a cream cheese pound cake. Would you like a slice?"

"Um, just a cup of water for right now please. If possible, can I get a rain check on the slice of cake. I wouldn't want to spoil my appetite before we have dinner." Sameer responded.

"Sure, you can get the slice of cake when you bring Keri back home later on tonight." Nana Carrie replied as she got up off the couch and made her way into the kitchen.

"Honey," Nana Carrie called out to her husband. "Can I get you anything?

Shaking his head no, Silas offered Sameer a seat.

"Thank you, sir." Sameer said, as he took a seat on the matching love seat, that was to the right of the couch.

Since their dinner reservations were not for another hour, Sameer and Keri along with her grandparents, caught up on the week's events concerning work, personal and happenings around the world. The conversation was with Keri and her grandparents were just like the ones he had with her on the phone; it just felt so right.

Before you knew it, it was time to officially begin their first date. Reaching to pick up her pocketbook off the sofa table, Sameer stood up and thanked Grandpas Silas and Nana Carrie for their hospitality. Kerri kissed both of her grandparents and said that she would be home in a couple of hours.

"Enjoy yourselves" Silas and Carrie said as Keri and Sameer made their way to his car.

After making sure she was seated and secure, he slid into the driver's seat.

"Are you ready?"

Looking at him and giggling, "Yes and again I want to thank you for agreeing to take me to my place of choice for this date."

"Are you kidding me? No thanks necessary. Not only am I glad that you suggested it but I have to say that I was thoroughly pleased or should I even say ecstatic when you told me where you wanted to go. I mean it is not every day you get to see some of your Gospel favorites all under the same roof." When Keri suggested they go to a gospel concert, the one held at Kings Dominion had already passed, so Sameer looked to make her wish come true. He was pleased when he got a notification on his Facebook page from Fred Hammond about the Festival of Praise tour that was coming to Richmond.

He went online and secured two VIP tickets to the concert that featured a few of both his and her favorite Gospel artists. Keri was pleased to hear that.

"Yes" she said to herself, smiling. "Now if he is a worshiper, I must have hit the jackpot." She remembered her pastor telling the young ladies that if the man they are interested in is not ashamed to worship God in public, then that man took his relationship with God seriously and was not putting on a show.

Their dinner was nice and the concert was wonderful. The sounds of praise filled the Altria Theater and Sameer and Keri were able to purchase new releases from the artists to add to their personal collections. Before going home, they stopped at Starbucks for lattes and some dessert pastries and continued with their observations and highlights of the concert. Seeing Keri to her door, Sameer wished Keri a good night and promised to talk with her later on the next day after service. And the conversations continued, along with more dates and the meeting of families and holiday get-togethers.

That lasted for years with the engagement six months later and the destination wedding with Sameer's father officiating and Grandpa Silas giving her away to Sameer. Keri established their own ministry that catered to single women with children and men in transition from incarceration as well as gave birth to a set of twin boys who resembled their dad and loved their mother tremendously.

Who knew that all this would happen? All from a Facebook like between two strangers. As Keri reread her words, she smiled and said a quick thank you to God for granting her the desires of her heart; a man who not only loved and cherished her but a man who was committed to God and lived a life to back it.

VIRTUOUS
By Nikki P. Serene

"Then desire when it has conceived gives birth to sin, and sin when it is fully grown brings forth death." - James 1:15 ESV

SUNDAY

Therese checked herself in the floor length, ladies room mirror one last time. Stepping back, she turned slightly to the side, getting a nice view of her full and shapely behind. She wore the traditional all-white uniform that was required of all the women there. But no one filled it out or wore it like Therese. The cool, soft cotton was just snug enough to show every curve of her body.

The skirt played with the imagination. You could see the outline of her tall, thick and sexy legs, leading the eyes down to her perfect feet in the perfect heels. Her blouse was tailored, maximizing her small inviting waist and her perfectly shaped large breasts. Her body was completely covered and yet her ensemble left everything to pleasurable imaginations.

She winked at her reflection in the mirror. The look was perfect. Her confidence was high and she was ready to catch the eye of her man. Her walk commanded the attention of every man and woman she walked past. Her look was perfection, her body flawless, and the smell of her perfume left even the strongest-willed; mesmerized as they followed her with their eyes.

Oblivious to the attention she drew, Therese walked past the others. The sound of the music ushered her in as a personal theme, in sync with her smooth stride. She found her usual seat close to the front. Her presence commanded the attention of everyone in back of her as well as everyone in front of her. Her eyes scanned in front of her until they were locked in with the eyes of her man.

Only Therese noticed the twinkle in his eye. He approved of her look. He loved her body and he loved the way she excited him. Her eye twinkled back at him. Anthony couldn't imagine his life without Therese. Therese was everything that he needed, everything that he wanted. And he wanted her, right then and right there.

He closed his eyes and listened to the music. He should get up now.

"Let us all stand and greet Pastor Anthony Bowles with a hearty amen." The hand claps and the 'amen's' brought him out of his trance. He opened his eyes and stole one last glance at Therese.

Anthony stepped up to the microphone. He opened his mouth to speak but he couldn't find his voice. Therese looked so good. He couldn't focus on the job at hand. Anthony knew how to play the game. He closed his eyes, lifted his hands high in the air and kept them there.

After a few seconds the organist caught on. The music shifted. Following his lead, the crowd also closed their eyes and raised their hands. Someone started the first hallelujah and the praise spread like a wildfire in California in dry season. That five minutes, was what he needed to compose himself.

He motioned for the usher to bring him some water. He didn't speak until after the crowd eventually settled itself down. Opening his Bible, he went to his prepared sermon. He needed to make this quick.

"Focus Anthony," he thought to himself.

He couldn't allow himself to get lost in his thoughts. His mind and body belonged to Therese. But his life belonged here. This church, it was like a readymade family that kept his life and his future enslaved. Anthony was struggling this morning. This was getting harder to do and impossible for him to love. The organist had stopped playing and the silence was unmistakably uncomfortable.

M'shelle lifted her head up toward Anthony. She hadn't noticed how long the silence had been. She looked back down at her phone and hit OKAY to send the text message she had been typing.

"Yes, Lord! Use him Jesus", she said out loud in a determined voice. M'shelle knew what to say to get him started. She didn't want to be in here all day.

At the sound of M'shelle's voice, Anthony snapped out of his trance. His wife knew how to bring him back.

"Let us all turn to the book of Matthew."

Back on track, M'shelle turned her attention back to her smart phone. She had already missed two text messages.

Text message one: "How long before you're are done"

Text message two: "R you going to be on time?"

She figured Anthony wouldn't be more than twenty minutes. He had been out almost all night. It was nearly dawn when he came home and crawled into the bed beside her. This morning she went into her home office and printed an older sermon off of her laptop. She slipped it in his Bible and left a handwritten note on top... "Sermon inside"

M'shelle's mind was really on her Sunday dinner. It was

being prepared by her personal chef and special friend. Chef titillated all of her senses. She shifted in her seat as she imagined what delights Chef had prepared for her.

Her husband was skilled. He knew how to work his crowd and how to do it quickly. She suspected that he was in just as much of a hurry to leave as she was. Within minutes, she heard her cue. Not only was M'shelle the First Lady of the Brooklyn House of Worship, she also served as missionary president, and oversaw the communion table.

Five ladies all dressed in white, followed behind her, folding the white sheet that covered the communion table and placing white gloves on the hands of all the ministers. Then they each took a station, one next to the musicians and four others near the elderly saints. They weren't expected to walk for the communion, so the women made sure they were served.

M'shelle had the communion structure down to a science. The entire church could be served the wafers and wine in about seven minutes. She only had to do her mandatory meet and greet and make her way to her car. Chef was waiting. And, she was ready for her Sunday treat.

Anthony noticed that his wife had been MIA every Sunday afternoon for the last seven weeks. She insisted that she needed private time to unwind. He also noticed that she rushing through this communion.

The Pastor and his Lady stood side by side at the entrance of the church, shaking hands, smiling. It was the perfect picture of a blessed couple. They wished everyone a good week and encouraged them to come back on Tuesday for Bible Study. After greeting the last parishioner, the painted smiles quickly left their faces.

"What time will you be home?"

M'shelle turned her face up. "I don't know. Did you need me for something?"

"I would like to see my wife sometimes."

"You had all last night to see me." M'shelle delivered

the verbal jab as she retrieved her purse.

"Your dinner is already prepared. Just turn the oven on for thirty minutes".

"So you're not eating with me, again?"

M'shelle felt her phone vibrate with another text. She answered her husband, "No. Just hold my plate to the side. If I don't get it tonight, I will take it to work, tomorrow." She had no intention of eating with Anthony tonight.

Anthony watched his wife get into her car. Why would she think he was going to sit home and wait for her to come back from wherever she was going? Not to be outdone, he reached in his pocket to pull out his phone. He sent the text as soon as she pulled away.

Meet me at my house in fifteen...

****

Therese hated the First Sunday more than any other Sunday. Standing next to M'shelle, taking her directions; had her stomach in a bundle of nerves. She considered stepping down from being a Missionary. Anthony didn't want to raise suspicions so he convinced her to serve in the same capacity that she always had. She parked her car close. She parked in the parking lot of the McDonald's on Atlantic Avenue. Sipping on her sweet tea she waited to hear from Anthony.

No matter how she felt on the inside, her demeanor remained cool calm and collected. She was admired by many for her classy ways. On the flip side, she was all but despised for being so sexy. Not that people didn't like her, they just didn't know what to do with her. Traditional church didn't have a place for sexy.

Anthony's text came through right when she expected. Therese started her Lexus and made a right turn out of the parking lot. Keeping straight down Atlantic, she headed toward Downtown Brooklyn. In exactly fifteen minutes, she pulled up in front of his Park Slope brownstone. She unlocked the door and Anthony got in the passenger side. He reached for her right hand and held it in silence until they crossed the Brooklyn Bridge into the city.

Therese spoke first. "I missed you baby"

Anthony leaned his head back on the head rest. "How much, baby? How much do you miss your man?"

Therese let go of his hand and began to gently rub his leg. "This much baby." With one hand on the wheel, she navigated her car toward the West Side.

"Mmm. That feels good." She knew how to relax him. "You looked so good today. I couldn't even get started preaching."

"Thank you, baby. You know I had to look good for you." She continued to rub his leg. It was sensual. Anthony wanted her.

The traffic was starting to slow down as they got closer to the Holland Tunnel. They crossed over into New Jersey. Therese pulled into the parking lot of Dunkin Donuts. Anthony took off his seat belt and unbuckled hers. He pulled her over to him and kissed her passionately. Her tongue found his and his hands ran down her back until her large soft behind was in the palm of his hand. She tasted so good, he wanted her right there in the car.

It would be about fifteen more minutes before they reached her spot in Newark.

****

Chef took M'shelle by the back of her head.

"Close your eyes baby and open your mouth." He took his fingers and opened her lips. They opened easily.

"Do you want it?" He whispered in her ear.

"Yes," M'shelle answered. This game was already beginning to excite her.

"Tell me you want it?" His deep voice was driving her

wild.

"Chef, baby, I want it"

Chef ran his fingers across her lips and M'shelle opened her eyes.

"No baby," He took his hand and gently closed her eyes. "No peeking". She moaned in anticipation.

Chef reached behind M'shelle and grabbed a handkerchief. He was really hoping she would try to peek because he wanted to make this fun. Standing over her, he blindfolded her. Her excitement built and she parted her lips to invite him in. He gazed down at the beautiful woman lying there. She was ready for him. He dipped a cold, sweet strawberry in the fondue pot that was full of warm, dark chocolate.

He placed the full sweet fruit on her full sweet lips. Her tongue reached to lick the sweet warm chocolate and she gently bit the tip. The sight of her tongue nearly sent Chef into a frenzy. He wanted to have her, to take her right there. Her mouth was opened again.

"Give me more, Chef." She was ready to beg for this.

He tried to regain his composure. He took another strawberry and rubbed it around her lips. The strawberry was so sexy and intimate. Her mouth opened wider for more. Chef found his hand caressing her smooth caramel skin. He leaned in and his lips found hers. He tasted the strawberry on her tongue.

She placed her hands behind him and pulled him in closer. He found himself dangerously close. He could feel the rises of her body. Her lips were sweeter than honey, full soft and inviting. At six foot five, Chef towered over most. His skin was smooth and dark. His head, clean shaved. His sexy muscular body was the grand production of his dedicated nights of weight lifting and cross fit training. He cooked healthy, he ate healthy. Strong, fine and confident, he conquered everything he put his hands on.

He slid his hands over the front of her crisp white

blouse. He caressed her breasts then slid the blouse over her head. Underneath her First Lady garb, M'shelle wore a sexy red strapless bra. He lifted her skirt and found that she also wore the matching red thongs. It had been eight weeks now that he was back in New York. For the last seven Sundays, he had M'shelle at his apartment for dinner.

They talked, they laughed, and they kissed and allowed the sexual tension between them to build. But this was the day that they would take this to the next level. M'shelle didn't just want Chef to have her; she wanted him to take her. She wanted to be engulfed in his every kiss and every touch. She needed this and she needed him, her knight in shining armor, delivering her from a life of frustration with Anthony to all of the excitement his body and his world had to offer. Her reality was in Chef.

For years, she missed him. For weeks, she longed for him. Nothing was going to stop this moment. Chef stripped M'shelle from the starched white, church garb. He removed her bra and thongs. She was still the most beautiful woman he had ever seen. He fell in love with M'shelle the first time he met her. He was twelve and had come to live with his grandmother after his mother and father lost custody of him. His grandma, affectionately called Mother Green, was a respected and revered mother at the Brooklyn House of Worship. M'shelle was the daughter of the pastor, Elder Jenkins.

Chef was nearly dragged into the small Sunday school room at the back of the church. Five other teenagers were already in there. But the only one he saw was M'shelle. Her body was slim but it showed all the graces of her growing womanhood.

"Welcome to our church." M'shelle was the first to stand up. She held out her hand to shake his, with a warm and sincere welcome.

At the age of thirteen, she was already sophisticated. He was impressed. No one had ever spoken to him with such respect.

"Thanks" he awkwardly shook her hand. He was used to giving a "dap" or a "fist pound" to people his own age. But M'shelle wasn't that type of girl.

"My name is M'shelle Jenkins".

"My name is Che.. I mean, my name is Charles David. Everybody calls me Chef" She didn't ask why.

"Nice to meet you, Chef. This is our Sunday School Teacher, Sister Jean and this is the rest of the group. Most of the people our age come later. They don't get up for Sunday school."

Chef nodded to acknowledge everyone else in the room and took a seat. He sat quietly.

"Damn this honey is fly" He winced as soon as he thought it, not sure if it was okay to think of curse words inside of church.

Chef earned his nickname early. His mom and pop never had enough sense to take care of him. He had to learn to cook early, that was the only way he would eat. Drugs, also known in the church community as "that crack demon" had possessed his parents' body and common senses. They didn't work and the monthly government money that came in was owed to the crack man long before they got it each month.

Tired of always being hungry, the young boy swiped and kept the food stamp card. At six, he learned to shop for food. He quickly graduated from cold cereals and ramen style noodles to burgers and hot dogs. Then, he met his hero. Chef Bobby Flay came to his school to tape a show for the Food Network. Young Chef was chosen as one of Chef Flay's helpers.

From that day, he knew his passion and his life was to cook, to be a famous Chef like Bobby Flay, get his own TV show and cook his way out the hood. After two years of being in the custody of the Administration for Children's Services, Chef was officially adopted by his grandma. She recognized his talent in the kitchen and added her own southern cuisine knowledge to his repertoire. By the time Chef was twelve, he was solely responsible for cooking Sunday and special occasion meals for the two of them and the guests that would come over.

M'shelle and Chef were friends from the start. The church recognized the budding romance between the teenagers. By the age of seventeen, Chef made the decision to ask her to marry him on her twenty-first birthday. Four years was not a long wait for true love. Chef may have been a "nice boy" but he was absolutely not the man that Pastor and First lady Jenkins had in mind for M'shelle.

They had taken good care to groom her from childhood to be in ministry. She would be the wife of a pastor. The Pastor and First Lady would not leave that to chance. Their radars had been out for years, always sizing up the sons of their clergy friends and associates.

Anthony was the youngest son of Elder Anthony Bowles Sr. and First Lady Martina Bowles from Holiness Church of God in Hempstead NY. He was raised "right" from the start. He had given his trial sermon at the age of thirteen and was licensed as a minister by seventeen. Young Anthony started evangelizing at other churches at the age of nineteen. He was a handsome preacher, in high demand as a preacher and as a prospective husband.

When the two pastors and first ladies met, the attraction between the two families was undeniable. Dating between Anthony and M'shelle was arranged. Marriage was the expected outcome. M'shelle wasn't rebellious, but her heart had always belonged to Chef. Their friendship and their attraction for each other grew. She was reluctant to date Anthony, especially the arranged meetings.

The winds of fate blew in favor of Anthony. Chef's grandma was very sick and was forced to go on retired disability. She had been battling breast cancer for two years. Chemotherapy and radiation removed the cancer but left her aged body weak. She had relatives down in Richmond VA, who arranged to have her and Chef to move out of the city. At the age of seventeen he could have stayed in NY, but leaving his beloved grandmother was not an option. She had been there for Chef when no one else was...and he wouldn't leave her, even though it meant that he had to leave M'shelle.

Fast forward eight years, his Grandma had passed away and Chef came back to Brooklyn for M'shelle. He finally had M'shelle tightly in his grasp, and he didn't intend to ever let her go, again.

****

M'shelle was intoxicated by the love making she just had with Chef. For hours, he kissed her, touched her and told her how much he loved her. Afterwards he held her and she drifted off to sleep. But, when she woke up during the night she realized that she was in the arms of Chef and not Anthony. She started to get up. Chef woke up when he felt her pull away.

"Where are you going baby?" Chef reached out to M'shelle and pulled her back into his arms. He wasn't ready to let her go.

"I should have been home hours ago."

"It's 1:30 in the morning. I'm not letting you leave out of here this late."

M'shelle reached for her phone. She imagined there were a flood of missed calls and messages from Anthony. He would be furious. To her surprise... no missed calls...no text messages.

"Wow" she said out loud.

"What is it?" Anthony took the phone from her hand and placed it on his side of the bed.

"He didn't call me at all. I guess he didn't come home,

again". M'shelle was hurt and confused. Ignored by her husband and loved by her lover.

Chef held M'shelle tighter, he wanted to protect her from the pain Anthony caused her. He kissed her forehead. "It's okay baby."

Chef stroked M'shelle's beautiful hair until she drifted back to sleep. He felt her struggling through her pain. She just wanted to be loved. He knew Anthony only married her for that church. He didn't love her like Chef did. Chef focused that he would never let Anthony get the chance hurt her again.

MONDAY

Therese arrived at her afternoon salon appointment. She kept up her weekly beauty rituals, making sure that her hair looked good for her man. Sitting under the dryer, she scrolled through her Facebook newsfeed; stopping on Anthony's page. He had just posted a color advertisement of the up and coming Annual District Conference of Churches. This year, the full week of church gathering, ordinations, officer appointments and gala celebrations would be held in Richmond. Months of planning sessions and organization went into the Conference.

The people who came were supporters of the ministry but they expected much in return. Guest preachers of great stature were invited, recording artists sang along with the choirs. All who graced the pulpit and podiums had one purpose, to preach and/or sing until the heavens came down. Therese felt her heart skip a beat when she saw the post. On the flyer, there was a perfectly posed picture of Pastor Anthony Bowles and his First Lady M'shelle Bowles.

Her man was a candidate for promotion; a District Elder

for the Conference, his wife would be promoted to the District's Women's Council of Missionaries and Evangelists. A natural reaction, her mouth formed a frown. "This is some bull…" she whispered to herself.

She was pissed. Of course she was aware of the annual conference but Anthony never once mentioned his great promotion. She scrolled through the comments. Already there were likes and comments, congratulating the young couple. Everyone wished them well and was praying for their success.

Therese was afraid. She could complete with M'shelle but she didn't know how she would complete with this. The position of District Elder would come with more responsibilities, a lot more than what he had going on at their church. He would be expected to travel, visit other churches, run revivals. He would be more popular and in higher demand. Of course, M'shelle was a part of the package. She would be expected to be at his side, at every church and every event.

Therese would have to make it clear that she was not to be neglected. She would have to fight harder. She imagined that Anthony would also be exposed to more women. Right now, she was the only one. A young fine preacher like Anthony was a prime catch for a lot of these desperate lonely women in church.

Knowing what she was up against, she sat up in the dryer chair. For the next thirty minutes, she discretely did her Kegel exercises, aggressively squeezing the muscles between her legs. She dropped and picked up an imaginary quarter with her kitty-kat.

"Tighten your stuff up girl" she thought to herself. She knew the exercises worked because she was already the perfect fit for Anthony. She would always be the perfect fit for him. Therese made sure that she would always be on top and left nothing to chance.

As her stylist combed out her wrap, Therese realized she

had squeezed herself horny. She sent a text to Anthony with a double meaning

"If U hungry like I am then U should be coming for me".

Anthony looked down at his phone. He half grinned at the text from Therese. As much as he gave her last night, she was still hungry for him. He was more than willing to satisfy her appetite.

"where R u," he texted back. He was eager to know what Therese was willing to offer.

"Downtown"

Therese lived in New Jersey but she spent most of her time in New York. She had a growing pediatric medical practice in Downtown Brooklyn, the church was right off Fulton in the heart of Bedford-Stuyvesant. For two nights a week she taught as an adjunct professor at MCNY in SoHo. Anthony dialed her number. It was too much to text, drive and watch out for NYPD. They were too quick to give out tickets for driving and being on the phone

"Hey baby" Therese answered the phone in a super sexy voice She knew how to make her man crazy.

"So, you're hungry baby?" He waited for Therese's answer. He loved when she talked sexy to him

"Mmm Hmm. I need to see you."

"Why", he asked. He knew exactly what she wanted, but he wanted to hear her ask for it.

"Nevermind." This was strike one. "I am heading back to Jersey. If you want me then come meet me, if not I'm out. I'm not waiting around to sit in traffic" Therese was horny but she wasn't about to lose her cool by begging.

"Relax baby, I got you". Anthony stopped the game quickly. He rarely turned down a chance to be with Therese. They both had busy schedules. "Meet me at the church. I'll be done in an hour."

Anthony took his time driving down Atlantic Avenue. He was headed to the church to conduct a pre-marital counseling session. He found it ironic that part of his job was to give counsel on how to have a good marriage. Anthony and M'shelle never sat through any counseling. But his father-in-law laid down the rules about twenty minutes before the wedding ceremony. It was simple but powerful: "The day you realize you don't want M'shelle anymore, send her back home." Funny thing is, after all of these years and even with their lifestyle, he never had any intention on sending his wife back.

Anthony glanced down at his phone. M'shelle didn't call or text all night. He knew she had been out all night. When he went home to shower and change he saw that nothing had been touched. She must have left for work from wherever she was. The thought of M'shelle doing her own thing put Anthony in a bad head space. Anthony rationalized the situation to himself, "She should have called me by now. I would have come home if she had called me home."

He had the sudden urge to speak to his wife. Pressing speed dial, he anxiously awaited to hear her voice. It rang five times then went to voicemail.

"Woman, where are you? Call me back!" he demanded on the answering machine.

Anthony parked in front of the church. M'shelle hadn't called him back. He didn't know what game she was playing. He didn't even know what game he was playing. But he did know that their life together would not last if they didn't get themselves together.

Anthony really felt like he just didn't matter to M'shelle. His wife was quality. Always had been. The first time he laid eyes on M'shelle, he was in awe. She had beautiful caramel colored skin, a flawless face, and a perfect body.

M'shelle intimidated Anthony from day one. When they met, he didn't have the gall to ask her on a date. He smiled remembering when they finally had their first date. His parents and her parents actually had to arrange for it to happen.

He picked M'shelle up at her house in Laurelton, Queens. From there, the ride to Juniors took about 30 minutes. He remembered being fascinated by the sound of her voice. They discussed during the ride, being a "PK" over dinner, and their own ministry goals over cheesecake. M'shelle was smart, experienced, she loved God and she loved ministry. She knew the Word. He knew from that first date that she was a keeper.

Everything he loved about her back then was what he still loved about her now. She was still smart, still beautiful and she was successful at work and church. People connected to her. Most of all, M'shelle could break down the Word and teach a class better than most, better than him really. Everything she touched worked.

Anthony snapped out of his thoughts as he saw the young engaged couple park behind him. They were smiling and laughing, eager for their pre-marital counseling.

Anthony checked his phone one last time. She still had not responded. This needed to be dealt with. He exhaled and sent a text to Therese.

"Babe, go ahead and head home, we will get up later this week."

The couple waved to Pastor Anthony as they walked past his car and up to the church. At that moment, Anthony knew exactly how he would advise them. "Always make sure you let each other know, just how much they matter."

****

Therese's heart sank as she read the text. Anthony told her to go home. Why did Anthony get to call the shots of when they did or did not get to be together? She hated for anyone to have that kind of control over her. After her hairdresser finished her hair, she made sure she refreshed her eyebrows and added a wax to remove any hair that might have started to grow on her upper lip. Looking in the mirror she reapplied her lip gloss before she left the salon.

Therese refused to answer Anthony's text. She was not giving him the satisfaction or even the opportunity to hear any weakness in her voice. She was mad at herself for even sending him the earlier text to meet.

"Every time I let my guard down this happens" Therese huffed to herself as she got into her car.

Looking in the mirror changed everything. Staring back at her was a scared, hurting and broken girl, a sinner who was destined to take her life straight to hell. She breathed deep to get control of her emotions. She was surprised to see a tear peeking out the corner of her eye.

"Therese, get yourself together," she scolded herself. One broken date was not that serious. "This is his loss. You are better than this."

She was never good in dealing with her emotions. When people looked at her now, they saw a strong, confident and well put together woman. But the truth was that no one could break through her wall that protected her heart. Anthony had yet to experience her cold side, the one who didn't forgive others for hurting her. If he was going to make it a habit of breaking dates, then her emotional walls would have to go back up.

Therese learned early in life how to turn her emotions on and how to quickly turn them off. She was the daughter of a crack addicted mother and an alcoholic father. Raising Therese was not a high priority on their list. She was always a beautiful girl, but it took years for anyone to know it. Therese was always "that girl". The broke girl, the girl without good clothes, the girl who was dirty, and the girl who had a bit of an odor to her.

People judged her without knowing that she was also the girl whose parents spent every dime on their addictions. Food, clothes, laundry, and soap were luxury items for her. She learned how to make do with whatever she had. Therese escaped her life by focusing on school.

She set an impossible goal to become a pediatrician. She poured herself into her studies at Brooklyn Tech High School. It was a successful plan that earned her straight "A" status and won a full scholarship to Virginia Commonwealth University in Richmond, Virginia. The eight years at VCU turned the fragile awkward young girl into a beautiful, confident and successful doctor.

Therese rolled down the window to her Lexus. She needed fresh air, and she needed to talk. She finally picked up her phone and called down to Richmond, to speak to her best friend, Jillian.

Jillian saw the 973 area code and grinned, "Hey, baby girl" Jillian answered.

"Hi sweetie," Therese answered. She was relieved Jillian answered. "I need my friend"

"What's going on?" Jillian sensed that there was some pain in her friend's voice.

Therese sighed, "Everything and nothing, is going on. I'm tired, I'm lonely, and right now I'm horny!"

Both of them burst out into laughter. The wall around Therese started to come down.

"Girl, I can't help you with being lonely or horny! You need Jesus!"

"I know I need Jesus and I need a man," Therese laughed back. "Are there any good ones down there?"

"Come visit so I can hook you up." Jillian always wanted Therese to visit.

"There is this really nice dude that joined the church a few months ago. He's the super trinity; fine, single and straight" Jillian taunted.

"And no one snatched him up yet?" They both knew how hungry the single women in church could be. "What's wrong with him? Matter of fact, don't tell me. I already have a man that's too much for me."

Jillian knew her friend was seriously dating but didn't know too much about the man. After months of dating,

Therese still kept him a secret. Jillian felt like something was wrong, but she had yet to put her finger on what it was.

"So what is wrong?" Jillian really was concerned.

Therese sighed again, "He broke a date. After I told him that I needed to see him, he sent me a bogus text to say he will get up with me later."

"Gotcha." Jillian was starting to get the picture. She knew just how Therese reacted when she faced rejection. That picture of a strong black woman, was only a picture.

Simultaneously, their minds went back about five years. Jillian was engaged to her husband and Therese was seriously dating a gorgeous young minister from Roanoke VA. Minister Chris Watson, was the most eligible church bachelor in the state. He kept Therese by his side and it was assumed by everyone that the two would be married and building a ministry together. Therese was so in love with the man and becoming his First Lady, that she nearly left medical school to follow him. He was a smooth charismatic, but Therese wasn't the only honey he was sweet talking.

They arrived together at the annual State Meeting of Churches. But, when Therese went to the ladies' room she found herself surrounded by no less than five women, who all claimed Minister Watson as their man. A physical fight broke out, the women jumped her and she landed in the hospital with a broken hand and a severed heart.

Chris found out about the fight and rushed over to Henrico Doctor's Hospital. In the ER, he told Therese that he was definitely in love, but it wasn't with her. He found that it was a perfect time to tell her that he was going to be a father by a young lady he met up in Alexandria. A wedding had been planned for the end of the month. Taking the cowards way out he told Therese, "God must have planned for this to happen so that I could finally tell you. This was in His will"

"Jilli" Therese snapped herself back to the present, "I

really am getting tired of these men in church"

Jillian understood. Therese really needed to know and experience the true love of Jesus. If she would ever let Him in, He would be enough. He would be all the love she needed because He would show her the greatest kind of love; self-love. But, she chose to not preach this time.

"When you're ready to meet this guy, let me know. And, make some time to get down here to visit" she added.

"I will soon, I promise. I love you, lady" Therese hung up, feeling a little better and a little stronger.

Heading back into Jersey, she decided to bypass Newark. She didn't want to be home alone. And, she definitely didn't want to be where Anthony could easily find her IF he should change his mind. Instead, she took the exit for the Garden State Parkway and headed toward Atlantic City.

****

Anthony needed to make sure he was still the man of his own home. He already knew he was the man at Therese's. For weeks, he had been losing touch with his own wife. There were two things he needed to make sure of. One, that she didn't suspect anything between him and Therese. And two, to make sure there wasn't another man in the picture. He needed solid answers tonight so he could get back in control.

"Did you eat yet?" Anthony sent a text to his wife. They needed some time together. He hoped that she would decide to answer this time.

Minutes later, she did. "Not yet. What are you wanting?"

"Meet me at BBQ's" he typed.

The popular couple arrived simultaneously and walked in the Downtown Brooklyn restaurant together. They were always the picture outward perfection. They could never predict when they'd would run into someone they knew or that knew of them. Anthony played his part as he pulled out M'shelle's chair with a tender touch.

He waited until the server had brought the drink order before he went in.

"So, what's going on with you?" Anthony asked.

"Nothing is going on with me." M'shelle took a long sip of her virgin strawberry daiquiri. She wished she could have ordered the real thing.

"Nothing? So, where were you last night? A wife doesn't disappear and stay out all night"

"Where were you Saturday night?" she asked without looking up. She wasn't about get thrown under this bus by herself.

Anthony glared at her. "I didn't bring you here to fight."

She didn't want to fight with him either. M'shelle let a moment of silence pass while flipping through the menu.

"Baby, I want a quarter rotisserie and an order of wings." She looked up from the menu and smiled gracefully. If he wasn't going to tell his secrets, she would be a fool to tell hers.

Anthony watched his wife. Weeks ago, she was so in love with him that she was hanging on his every word. If he wanted an ego boost he could ignore her and watch her beg for his attention. Now she was acting as if he didn't exist. There was too much invested in this marriage. He always remembered that the church was M'shelle's. If they ever parted, he would be the biggest loser.

He shifted the conversation. "So this weekend, you become the wife of a District Elder"

"Yes baby! I'm excited" Changing the subject eased the tension.

"When are you going to be finished packing our clothes. Deacon Lyle can put them in his truck early. I asked him to drop us off at LaGuardia Saturday Morning."

The server arrived with a platter full of the crunchy

signature wings, ribs, rotisserie chicken and golden cornbread.

"Probably Wednesday." She reached over for his hand. Anthony blessed the food. This atmosphere seemed like the perfect recipe for the couple to reconnect.

TUESDAY

Tuesday night prayer and Bible Study was a constant in the lives of Pastor Anthony and First Lady M'shelle Bowles. Early in their ministry, they found it was best to take turns. He prayed and taught the church on the 1st and 3rd Tuesdays, M'shelle on the 2nd and 4th. In the event there was a 5th Tuesday in the month, they held a joint bible class that focused solely on family. The strongest and most admired trait of any young couple in ministry was consistency.

For M'shelle, this Tuesday came too quick. It was her turn to minister. Just two days ago she was in the arms of her lover, enveloped in ecstasy and desire. It was just after four o'clock when M'shelle parked in front of the church. She had three short hours to get her head out of the clouds and prepare the lesson for the night. One of the older deacons, Deacon Lyles already had the church open. He met her at the car to secure her to the building.

'Praise the Lord, First Lady" Deacon Lyles helped M'shelle out of the car.

"Praise the Lord, Deacon Lyles" M'shelle genuinely smiled. "How are you today?"

"I am blessed and highly favored" he proclaimed. The Deacon was a faithful member for over forty years. He proudly served in ministry under her father and now under her husband. He loved his church and his church family.

Deacon Lyles helped M'shelle with her rolling case. It housed her laptop, two bibles and several books of biblical study material. He chatted about his children and grandchildren. She was relieved when they made it to her office.

"Thanks Deacon"

"Don't mention it First Lady. I am here to serve" He rolled the bag in and quickly made his exit out of the room.

The First Lady's church office was her mecca of peace inside of the busy church building. The space was a combination of her mother's old office and an unused classroom. When M'shelle was officially installed as First Lady, the renovated office was a gift from her mother to her. The two room suite served its purpose well. The outer office allowed her to take visitors.

It was there where she counseled and talked with her parishioners. The decorated walls told a story of two generations, framed pictures of her father, mother, the church and the older saints that founded the church. She found that it was the inner office that she enjoyed the most. Few had ever been allowed in that personal space. It was sanctified, set apart from the rest of M'shelle's world. It was her place to pray, to study, to meditate and seek God. M'shelle could spend hours in her inner office, often unaware of the passing of the time.

Today the office felt cold to M'shelle.

"I don't belong here" she whispered to herself.

She knew that she had to push through, but first and foremost, she needed to get a connection with God in order to find herself. Ever since Chef came back into town, she found herself spending more and more time with him, and less and less time with Him. The real issue was that she loved every minute of her time with Chef. She dimmed the lights in the room and pulled the pillows from the sofa onto the floor. She got on her knees and closed her eyes.

"Jesus" she called out. "What in the world have I done?"

M'shelle spent the next forty-five minutes on her knees, seeking the Lord until she found Him. She prayed and cried until she felt a breakthrough.

By 7:10pm, the church was about seventy-five percent filled. The joyful noise overtook the atmosphere. M'shelle having already reached her high point, prayed and exhorted the crowd. She used the cordless mike as she walked up and down the aisles of the church. She was caught up in a seventh heaven and speaking in other tongues. The synergy of her praise and the prayers and cries of the church shifted Tuesday night service into an extraordinary place of worship.

Chef had arrived at the church about 7:15pm. He could hear M'shelle halfway down the street. It sounded like they were having a time in prayer. He stepped in the dimly lit sanctuary and was taken aback by the praise that had filled the temple. He decided not to get on his knees but to quietly worship in his seat.

Chef watched M'shelle as she walked up and down the aisle of the church. He really came tonight simply to look on her beauty and to try to convince her to replay the events of Sunday. But, she was on fire. So much so, that Chef found his eyes closed and his mouth parting with his own quiet worship. M'shelle's powerful soprano voice seemed to be leading everyone in the church to the very Throne of Grace.

The crescendo of praise soon died down, the ceiling lights were turned back on and the Bible study portion of worship began.

"Let us turn to the book of Jeremiah." Chef smiled to himself. He was so proud of his woman, up there teaching with authority. She was smart, beautiful and sexy. He really needed her again tonight. Just before he slipped out of the sanctuary, he sent a text to her phone. When she finished teaching, he hoped she would see the message.

M'shelle saw the text. Before she could respond, Anthony had whisked her away home.

Anthony lay back on the bed, watching his wife pull of

her clothes. She knew what he was expecting, but the prayer and teaching had taken everything out of her. She welcomed her bed. She spooned with her husband and quickly fell asleep in arms.

WEDNESDAY

It was 5:30 in the morning. Anthony turned his head toward the bright green display, in the dark room. He had been awake all night, envisioning M'shelle from the night before. Her beauty was so natural; it was like her glow came from God. Her light perspiration across her forehead, her caramel skin had turned deep apple red. Her grip on the microphone was strong and she had pushed forward until the entire church was caught up on the same level of worship that she was in.

Thinking of this turned Anthony on. He sat up slightly and watched his wife sleep. He had been holding her all night, wanting to touch and be inside of his wife. He felt his manhood shift. He reached out his arms and pulled her toward him.

M'shelle woke up to the familiar touch of her husband's hands. She didn't fight the pull. She allowed herself to melt back into his strong masculine embrace. Anthony stroked his wife's beautiful hair. He was so turned on and he needed to make sure she was ready. He slid his hand down her back and in between her thighs.

After a few seconds, M'shelle gave in and opened her legs for him. She buried her head on his chest while he rubbed her body awake. She reached down to grip her hard husband and slid her hand back and forward.

"Yeah baby girl. Just like that" he instructed her. When he was ready, he pulled her legs up around his chest.

"Ah" M'shelle's moans filled the room. Her body shook when he pushed inside her.

M'shelle gave high pitched moans that sent Anthony wild. He spun her around and took her from the back.

"Talk to me baby" he wanted to hear her voice. "You like this baby?"

"Oh yes. Oh baby yes!"

"Yeah you like when I hit it like that". He went in harder.

"Yes baby." M'shelle rocked back and with her husband. But he was starting to get rough. Her thoughts wandered to Chef. She imagined how good it would feel to have him inside of her.

"Come for me baby" Anthony's voice pulled her from her thoughts of Chef.

"Come for me" he demanded. Anthony grabbed her shoulders and pushed harder.

"Mmmm" , she moaned for him.

"Oh yeah." Anthony flipped her back around. He stayed inside her until he felt her come. His body finally gave in to an explosive finale. He froze in position until he could regain some strength.

M'shelle slid out the bed. She felt a twinge of guilt for enjoying her husband. Anthony wanted to pull her back in, but decided against it. He was already too hot from putting in work. He watched his wife walk out of the room, and one thought stayed in his head.

Somebody else was getting his wife off. He knew every inch of her body. The normally tight fit just didn't feel right anymore.

Later that morning....

"Can you meet me at the restaurant?" He sent her the text early before she could make other plans. Chef was already disappointed that M'shelle didn't come to stay with him last night.

When Chef came back to New York, he made the decision to open a restaurant in Harlem. His blessing was a small turnkey restaurant for rent on 126th street. It was a transformed brownstone that utilized the parlor and first floors for business. The restaurant was steps away from Refuge Temple and from the State Building.

He flooded the neighborhood with menus. He even personally went to the church to introduce himself to the staff. He had always admired Apostle William L. Bonner and the work he had done in the Churches of our Lord Jesus Christ, Inc. When they lived in Richmond, his grandmother had raised him up in the organization.

The trendy Harlem neighborhood welcomed Mattie Renee's. He named the restaurant after the two loves of his life; his grandmother Mattie and his heart M'shelle Renee. In a few short weeks, he built a strong lunch crowd from the State Building. The dinner crowd picked up around six o clock and stayed strong throughout the night. The weekends were a blast. The upscale soul restaurant had guests from Harlem and around the city.

M'shelle saw the text and smiled. Today was M'shelle's busiest day this week. Her full time schedule began with work from 7 to 3 in the city, an hour-long trek on the A train to Brooklyn. From there, she picked up her car, and then took a hectic drive down Atlantic Avenue, avoiding potholes and gypsy cabs.

Today, M'shelle had two women on her counseling schedule. One had been coming to see her for nearly three months. She was a single, beautiful young lady that had been struggling to understand her sexuality. The second woman was an older woman who had recently lost her husband. She was raising three teenagers, two boys and a girl. She was overwhelmed, tired, and not understanding "why God had taken her husband from her."

M'shelle poured herself into the counseling sessions. She had received her online degree from Liberty University for Christian Counseling. She was also the daughter of a Pastor. This is what came with the territory. As a woman in position, it was natural that people drew to her for advice. It was her job to hear what God had to say, and to advise honestly and scripturally.

Both sessions were over by eight o'clock. She headed into her back office and made a cup of tea with her Keurig. She poured so much of herself into both women. For the second time that week she was physically drained from church. Sitting at her desk, she checked her phone for messages. Chef had sent a text.

"I left the door unlocked for you. How long will you be?"

A shiver ran through M'shelle's body. His touch was everything she wanted. She knew she was falling deeply in love with him. But her life was still here, behind the doors of this church. She was tired and had thought about cancelling with Chef. M'shelle picked up the phone. Instead of calling Chef, she made the call to Anthony. If he was home, she would go to him. If he wasn't, well…

"Hello" Anthony answered after the fourth ring.

"Hello, husband." She sensed in his tone that something was off. "Where are you?"

She was right. Anthony was in the bed of his lover. Therese draped her thick legs over Anthony and he almost lost calm composure.

"I'm with the guys. We came out to Jersey to pick out some new clergy shirts. It's going to be late before I get back"

M'shelle knew that he was lying. Tonight, she didn't care. His lies made her decision for her.

"It's already late. You should just stay out there. I don't like you driving sleepy."

Anthony rolled over on top of Therese. He put a finger to her lips to signal for her to keep quiet. She reached up and kissed him quietly. "I probably will. It's late already.

I'll see you tomorrow"

M'shelle hung up the phone. "He is so full of it" she said out loud.

"I am on the way." She replied to Chef's text.

"I am not going to keep sharing you with him" Chef looked M'shelle directly in her eyes.

M'shelle squirmed to get from under Chef's embrace.

"You aren't sharing me" she protested. "You make it sound like I'm sleeping with both of you. I told you already, he hasn't touched me." Her own lies made her uncomfortable.

Chef sat up in the bed. He was a man of few words. "First of all, I'm not a fool. Second, I wasn't talking about your body. I am talking about you."

"What about me? You have me here now"

"I'm talking about everything woman. I want your life, your love, your body, and your presence." Chef needed M'shelle to understand. He didn't come back to New York to be her side lover. He came back to get the love of his life. This had to be an all or nothing deal.

M'shelle maneuvered his arms to get back under his embrace.

"Baby, what do you want us to do now? You want me to leave him?"

"Yes" Chef was straight and to the point.

"So, I show up at your door with my clothes and then what? We couldn't stay in New York. The church would crucify me." M'shelle shuddered at the thought of her secrets being exposed. The church could be an unforgiving group. If this got out, it would take years to rebuild her reputation.

"Yes, we stay right here. I am not running because of church people's opinions."

"What about my ministry? That has nothing to do with Anthony. I still teach, and preach, and minister to women."

"I'm not asking you to give up any of that. I still want

you to teach and preach. You know how sexy you were on Tuesday? I saw you walking up and down that church shaking your thick behind." He gently smacked her on the backside.

"I saw the text but I didn't know you came to church Tuesday" The thought of Chef being that close to Anthony made her feel sick.

"Yeah, you walked right past me. You were so caught up." Chef kissed M'shelle. "You are so sexy, so beautiful."

M'shelle moaned at the sound of his voice. Chef began stroking her body. Her reaction to his touch told him everything he needed to hear. She was his. And he wasn't letting her go.

Chef moved himself on top of her. With all intensity and seriousness, he made love to M'shelle. His strong arms twisted her body in every position she had ever craved and imagined.

"Do you love me" She asked in his ear.

He kissed her hungrily as his stroke stayed consistent. "Yes baby. And, I know you love me, right?"

"I love you so much baby"

"Then choose me. Choose life with me." He began to stroke with intensity. He wasn't letting her go.

It was too much for M'shelle. First Anthony, now Chef. "Slow down baby"

Not speaking, he kissed her again. He didn't let up on his stroke.

"Baby, slow it down".

Chef was only going to stop, if she said to stop. But he had no intention of slowing down. M'shelle was in for a long, powerful night.

He felt so good inside of her. Chef's body spoke for him and it told M'shelle all the right things. He loved her with no strings attached. She couldn't let him go either.

For Therese, the phone call was perfect timing. Anthony would stay with her tonight. His promotion to District Elder was only days away. She had to put everything into this night; heart, soul and body. She needed to make sure Anthony needed her as much as she needed him.

"I have an idea baby" Therese cooed in Anthony's ear as she stroked the muscles on his tight chest.

Anthony returned the favor by stroking her soft huge breasts. "What is it baby?"

"Take me with you to Richmond."

He pinched her nipple, hard. "Why would you ask me that? I'm going with my WIFE to the convention" It was a ridiculous request.

Therese gasped from the pleasurable pain of the pinch. "I don't mean like that. I meant, that I thought of a way that I can go too"

"You are on the verge of pissing me off," he warned. Anthony got serious when he rolled top of Therese and put his hand around her neck. "Are you trying to ruin me?"

"No baby." She shook her head to try to loosen his grip. "No I just meant that I could go down also, if you appoint me as your executive secretary."

Anthony loosened his grip slightly. "You want to be my secretary. You're a doctor, and you want to run behind me to be a secretary?" Therese was sounding needy, and needy is never sexy.

"I want to be your secretary, baby. We can make it work. We can travel together and it would be ok" She reached down and grabbed his manhood with the same intensity that he had around her neck.

That move intrigued Anthony. "Hmmm. convince me"

Therese reached up and kissed him. She guided his hands off her neck to the back of her head. "Let me show you baby. You ready for this interview?" she slid from under him and maneuvered him on his back.

Anthony's body got rock hard. "Yeah, this is your interview." he played along with the game. "I was going to hire my wife"

Therese kissed her way down Anthony's body. "Oh really? So does she do this? She pulled his hard manhood in with her seductive mouth.

"Oh YEAH!" Anthony struggled to keep his composure. Oral was the one thing M'shelle didn't like to do. But Therese, wow! Her mouth and her tongue was like gold.

Therese knew she had her man's full attention. Anthony loved it when she went down on him. She slid her mouth from the tip all the way down. Therese knew M'shelle rarely did this for him.

Anthony put his hand on top of her head and pushed her down further. He loved the feeling of controlling her movements.

"Mmm hmm. You like that baby. I know you do" she said as she came up for air. Before he could respond, she went back down. Therese put on her show.

For thirty minutes straight, Therese delighted her man's body with every trick she had in her book. She would take him to edge and ease him back down. She knew when he couldn't hold it anymore. She went in full force; hands, tongue, mouth and breasts. She didn't let up until after he exploded and she had drained every drop out of him.

"Am I hired?" she asked coyly

Anthony pulled her up beside him. "You think I'm leaving all that behind?" he collapsed back on the pillow. "Friday, we can drive down in your car."

THURSDAY

For the second time that week the couple was at home together. Anthony had waited at home for M'shelle to get off of work. He sat on the bed and watched her begin to pack their bags for the weekend.

"I'm going to head down to Richmond in the morning." Anthony said the words as easily as he would have if he were going to the corner store.

M'shelle stopped packing and looked at her husband as though he had lost any good sense he might have had.

"Our tickets are for Saturday morning. We can't change them this close to the flight." She rolled her eyes at him. She didn't need this. She was already on the fence about going. Now Anthony was throwing another wrench in the gears.

"I'm going to drive. You are still flying in on Saturday. I will pick you up at the airport." Anthony's instructions were clear. He expected M'shelle to be compliant.

"Who are you driving with, Anthony". Her antennas were up, anticipating the lie he was about to tell.

"I'm going to pick you up when you get there." He didn't answer her question.

M'shelle rolled her eyes again. "Yeah, whatever Anthony"

"Come here" He reached out for her. When M'shelle didn't respond, he grabbed her and held her in a strong grip.

"Let me go" she squirmed trying to her best to get from under him.

"Let you go where?" He put his face in hers. "Stop moving" he demanded.

"Please let me go. I'll stop moving." M'shelle pleaded. She didn't want this to get physical.

"Stop talking so much." He loosened up a bit. "Your husband is right here holding you and all you want to do is walk away."

M'shelle rolled her eyes at him again. He responded with a gentle kiss on her lips. She felt his manhood pressing against her

The kiss was unexpected. "Is this what you want?" She

asked in a quiet, sensual whisper. She reached down and cupped Anthony's growing penis with her hand. She felt whorish. Why was this the only way to get his attention.

"Yeah, don't stop that." He let her massage it until he was rock hard. Still holding her, he scooped M'shelle up and lifted her onto the bed.

He rubbed his hands between her legs, preparing her body for his entrance. M'shelle began to moan. She moved her body to the rhythm of his hand.

M'shelle got serious. "This is what you want?"

Anthony turned on his back and lifted her on top of him. "Yeah baby, this is what I want"

M'shelle started her ride. She put everything into it. So much was at stake. She licked her lips. "Yeah, I know you want this...now."

"Baby, I always want you."

His answer made her angry. M'shelle rode him harder. "No. You don't always want me. I'm not your flavor".

Anthony was stiff as a rock. He treated this like a game and he liked it.

"Yeah, baby. You're my flavor. Come here." From the bottom position he took control of the ride. M'shelle bounced up and down on him at his will.

M'shelle watched her husband as he came down off his high. That ride was one hundred percent for him. If she had any chance of keeping her husband she would have step her game up. Make him realize that he didn't need other women.

"If he still leaves after this, then I am really finished" she thought.

As if on cue, Anthony got up. M'shelle quietly watched Anthony pack a small bag. Their love making didn't make a bit of difference or change his mind from leaving. It was apparent to her that she was not enough, and would never be enough for her husband.

She was ready to give up everything she had waited on

and worked for. All of it was at her door, but she was going to let it go. She silently decided that she would not show up in Virginia. Now, she couldn't wait for Anthony to leave. She wanted to call Chef and let him know. From now on, she would be his and his alone.

FRIDAY

Therese was waiting on the platform to meet Anthony when he arrived on the Path train from NY to Newark Penn Station. She knew how to keep her man happy by arriving early and being impeccably sexy. As soon as they stepped outside, she handed him the keys to her Lexus.

The six hour ride on 95South was smooth. Traffic was light. Anthony loved the way this was working out. Therese was at his side. M'shelle would be here tomorrow. He even toyed with the thought of having them together one day. He made a mental note to bring that up at a later time.

"Wait here baby," Anthony parked the Lexus in front of the Richmond Airport Double Tree hotel.

Therese nodded. She was excited to be back in Richmond. Plus, she was with her man. If he was willing to bring her here this week, then maybe the District Elder promotion wouldn't be that bad.

"Good afternoon sir. Are you checking in?" The cute desk clerk greeted and smiled at the handsome guest.

"Yes last name, Bowles. First name, Anthony." he leaned in and smiled.

She checked the computer. "Yes sir. A King Room." She looked closer at his face and she recognized him. This was the fine preacher from New York. He and his wife were the guest speakers at the Virginia Central Diocese Conference a couple of years back.

"Yes darling, a King Room."

The young woman stayed professional. She never hinted

that she knew him. She was like that with all of her guests whether a pilot, celebrity or even a preacher, all of the guests deserved privacy and anonymity.

"Room 313, sir" She handed him the room key and one of the warm signature chocolate chip cookies.

He leaned in and read her name tag aloud "Thank you, Jillian. Do you know what is better than one of these cookies?

"No sir" she answered.

"Two of them." Anthony winked. Jillian grinned and handed him a second cookie.

"Have a good afternoon and thank you for choosing the Double Tree Hotel"

Jillian watched him as he walked back out to park his car. Settling back in her chair, she grabbed a cookie to nibble on. She watched him on the security camera as he entered back in the hotel at the side door near the elevator. What she saw next made her fall out of the chair.

Unmistakably, that was not his wife he held the door for. That was her best friend Therese, and she was walking in with that gorgeous and married preacher.

****

Chef still had a business to run. He had his kitchen staff to arrive early in order to prep for a busy Friday. He also had to prepare for the weekend.

There was a full lunch crowd at Mattie Renee's. The deacons and missionaries at Refuge Temple were in planning meetings all day. Chef had prearranged a special prix fixe lunch so the saints could take their lunch break there. Lunch orders for delivery to the State Building were being called in back to back. Success was sweet and Chef was grateful. He wished that M'shelle was with him right now. He envisioned how it could be when she came to be with him. They would work side by side in the day, and love each other during the night.

The crew in the back of the house hustled at their individual stations. He had cooks on the fryer and pantry and his sous chef worked the grill. The Expo ensured that every table received food that was hot, visually appealing, and that it all arrived at the same time. Chef overlooked the entire production, and made sure his crew kept ticket time down to a strict ten minutes.

The saints fell in love with the restaurant at first sight. The building was a short walk from the church. The décor reflected a refined southern style kitchen. Chef made sure that his restaurant pleased all of the senses. The décor reflected a refined southern style restaurant; background music played a light mix of traditional and urban gospel music. On Sundays, the flat screen televisions that lined the walls broadcasted the Word Network with preaching and singing. The aroma of the food greeted guests as they entered into the foyer.

No one noticed the grungy couple that had been staking out the restaurant most of the week. They casually walked past the window and saw the place was packed. The timing for everything was right. When they got to the corner, they turned back around and headed to the mark.

"Let's go." The woman ordered the man. She was at least two steps ahead of him.

The man sighed without talking back. He dutifully caught up to her.

"Fool, you better be ready. We aren't turning back from this" She peered straight in his eyes.

"Yeah" he said. He patted his pocket where his gun was hidden. He was ready but not one hundred percent willing. "Are you sure this is it?"

They stopped in front of the door.

The woman smiled. The teeth that she had left in her mouth were blackened. "Yeah, I'm sure." She pushed open the door to Mattie Renee's and walked in with her head held high.

The hostess, Josette, quickly greeted the dirty couple at the door.

"Good Afternoon and welcome to Mattie Renee's" she had a nervous smile on her face.

The woman didn't answer back. She eyeballed Josette. A couple of the saints looked up but quickly turned their attention back to their meals.

Josette was a little unnerved by the couple. She made a motion for one of the male servers to come to the door. When he got there, she continued the conversation.

"I would be happy to get you both something to eat" she informed them. "Would you like that?"

"Girl, I don't want any of your food. The woman spat the words out. "Get your boss out here"

"Is there something I can help you with? We are pretty busy right now. My boss is in the kitchen." Josette answered. She looked to the server to speak up.

The server stepped closer toward the man. "What do you want? Because you can't stay here"

The woman rolled her eyes and looked towards her partner. "Check this fool!" she demanded.

The man reached in his pocket and pulled out the gun. He didn't say a word.

Josette and the server froze. "Oh God" she moaned. She couldn't believe it. They were going to be robbed right in daylight with all these guests.

"Go get your boss" The woman repeated.

Josette nodded toward the server. "Go get him, please"

The man put the gun back in his pocket. Clearly they weren't here to rob the restaurant.

In a few seconds, the server was back out with Chef on his heels. They both glanced at the guests in the restaurant. No one seemed to notice any problems. Chef smiled as he hurried through crowd and headed toward the front door.

"Thank you Josie" he motioned for his hostess to step away. He would find a way to diffuse this before it turned into a situation. He didn't want anything going down in the restaurant.

"I would love to help you both but I need you to step outside" Chef tried to lead them out the door. "Are you hungry?"

"We aren't hungry. We need some money, CHARLES" The woman emphasized Chef's first name.

Chef froze and looked at couple. He couldn't believe what he saw. "Ma, Dad, is that you?"

****

M'shelle had let go of her doubts about Chef. She smiled as she packed a good portion of her clothes. She would move in with Chef while Anthony was gone.

"I choose you. Text me when you finish at the restaurant."

She sent Chef the text with the answer he had been waiting for. Once she finished packing, she headed out to the salon to get a fresh do for her man. She would wait for him to text her back before she headed up to Harlem.

The Dominican hairdresser seemed to have magic in her fingers. Exhausted over the emotions of the week, M'shelle fell asleep in her chair and then back to sleep while she was under the dryer. The woman shook her awake.

M'shelle smiled, a little embarrassed. She wondered if she was snoring.

Checking her phone, she wasn't surprised that Chef hadn't returned her text. She knew he was busy but she imagined that he would be thrilled to hear that she was coming.

M'shelle sent another text. Perhaps he didn't get the first one.

"I am coming to you baby. Hit me up when you get

this."

An hour later and there was still no answer. It was almost five o'clock, just before dinner and a typically slow time in the restaurant. She decided to call.

"No answer still," M'shelle said to herself. She hung up deciding not to leave a message. She was getting a weird feeling in her stomach. It wasn't like Chef to not answer her.

For the next hour, she window-shopped at the Macy's downtown. There was still no word from Chef. Disappointed, she went to her car and decided to go back home.

SATURDAY

M'shelle woke up and reached for her phone. Chef didn't call or text. She couldn't believe that he had changed his mind about her.

She dialed his number again. *"Please answer baby. Don't leave me hanging like this"*

Again, M'shelle got the voicemail. The message she was getting from Chef was loud and clear. He didn't want her. She got up and called Deacon Lyles to pick her up.

The early Saturday morning traffic was nonexistent when Deacon Lyles dropped of the First Lady at LaGuardia Airport.

She sat at the gate, waiting for boarding. She was confused and hurt on so many levels. M'shelle quietly prayed for a sign or an answer. It was obvious that she was not wanted, not anymore. Anthony did not have to walk out, and Chef didn't have to ignore her.

M'shelle picked up her phone again. Chef still had not text her. She tried her best to keep her composure, she didn't want her tears to fall in the airport.

"Baby, why won't you text me or call me back?" she

thought. She needed her man. M'shelle was in the one place she didn't want be...heading back to be with Anthony.

The gate attendant had already seated the first class passengers. She sent one last text before she gathered her belongings for boarding.

"Baby I haven't heard from u. my heart is broken. All I want is to be in ur arms right now. But I guess your decision about us has changed. I am on my way to Richmond to continue my life. But my heart and my love are yours and will always be"

The line moved slowly toward the gate. The overhead television played the morning news. She watched the traffic report and was grateful for Deacon Lyles' promptness.

She took another step toward the gate agent. At least ten passengers were in front of her.

"Police are continuing to investigate yesterday's bold daytime shooting and robbery in Harlem."

M'shelle glanced back up the television screen. They were talking about a shooting in Harlem. The pictured area on the screen was all too familiar.

"That is near Chef" she thought. Looking back down at her phone, there was no response from Chef. The knot she already had in her stomach got tighter.

She read along on the teleprompter at the bottom of the screen as she listened to the newscaster.

"The owner of the popular new restaurant Mattie Renee's was robbed and shot twice in the chest yesterday in a daring daytime assault. Charles David, who is popularly known in the neighborhood as Chef, is still in critical condition at Bellevue Hospital. Police are asking anyone with any information on this to contact them."

M'shelle froze as she saw the picture of Chef across the screen. Critical Condition. The blood rushed from her head.

The young woman in the boarding line was proud of herself for paying attention. She noticed that the pretty young woman in front of her, seemed to be disturbed by something. Reacting quickly, she caught M'shelle as she passed out, and kept her head from slamming on the floor.

****

Anthony left the hotel early. He headed for the rental care area of the airport. They would still need their own way around since Therese drove her car.

He pulled the rented Kia Optima into one of the temporary parking spaces designated for picking up passengers. He walked over to the baggage area and waited for M'shelle to come down the escalator.

After all these years, and after everything that was happening between them, he was still always happy to see her. He smiled as he thought about how much he really missed her. They had only been apart for a day.

Passengers were coming downstairs but he didn't see M'shelle. It was unlike her to keep him waiting. She also had the type of presence about her that kept her in the front of the crowd.

Anthony waited for another fifteen minutes. He dialed her cell phone and it went straight to voicemail. This was unlike her.

"Excuse me" Anthony found a desk agent. "My wife is M'shelle Bowles. She has a ticket for this flight but I haven't seen her. Can you check?"

The policy of the airline was that passenger information was private. There was little she could confirm about his wife. Looking at the flight notes on the computer she was able to clue him in on some news.

"I cannot say for sure if this is her or not. But there was an incident at LaGuardia Airport. A passenger on this flight was rushed to the hospital with a possible heart attack"

For the first time in many years, Anthony burst into tears and bawled like a baby.

ECHOES OF THE HEART: DECEPTION (PARANORMAL LOVE)

By Tracy Mclean

It was 2:00am. I woke up in a cold sweat with my covers soaked, as if I had taken a dip into Lake Lanier and jumped back into bed. Darkness plagued my room and all the sound stood still. It was so dark. I couldn't see my hands in front of my face. Suddenly, a cold blast of air caressed my face. I felt as if my lips were touched. With each blasts of cold air, there was another caressing feeling. The water that dropped from the shower head echoed throughout my bedroom.

drip drop~ drip drop~ drip drop.

I laid still as I could, this feeling was amazing. I wish I could feel this good all the time. Then I felt my bed move with a little jolt as if there were someone joining me tonight.

"Carter," I said with anticipation in my voice. "Carter? Is that you?" Knowing that I wouldn't receive an answer, I continually called out for him.

You see, Carter is my fiancée' whom completed three years in Afghanistan. He served his country with pride and wanted so much to provide for his family with everything he had in him. Carter came home in June for Father's Day and for the birth of our first child (his son). I remember it as if were yesterday. Yes, yesterday.

I remember going into labor at 2:00 a.m. and telling Carter to call the ambulance. It was the strangest thing, he was so happy and then he was sad. First he paced the floor then Carter's face lit up like a light bulb. He kept a huge smile on his face and whatever I asked, he did.

"Kayla, I will meet you at the hospital. I am going to drive my own car and I will bring your things with me," he said with excitement and a little nervousness in his voice.

I replied "Ok," then Carter kissed me on my cheek and gave me a hug. I remember he held me so tight. He said he loved me so much then the ambulance whisked me away. That was the last time I would see my Carter. The doors shut to the ambulance and sirens blared loudly. I just remember thinking how much I loved this man.

When I arrived at the hospital, I was whisked away to the delivery room for hours. There were a lot of contractions and pain, but no Carter. After six hours, I had only dilated 3cm's and still no Carter. Where was he? I called his phone over and over again, wondering what had happened to him but still no answer. At this point, it had been over fifteen hours and no Carter.

Maybe he decided a baby was too much for him, but he seemed as if he loved the idea of having a kid, a son at that. I was so confused now.

At the eighteen hour, 8 p.m. sharp, I gave birth to; Carter Atrelle-Thomas Lane II. As the doctor placed him in my arms and I heard the beautiful sound of his cry, at that particular moment, I realized we were now a complete family. All of a sudden, there was a cold blast of air and a flicker of the lights. Then I heard a voice say, "Son I love you so much and only if I knew then what I know now" Brusquely, the door opened and shut to my room.

The voice spoke again, "I love you so much Kayla! But

why? Tell me why?" the voice asked with a tremble.

"Why what?" I said. Then with my tired eyes, I scanned the room for Carter but there was no sign. Still exhausted from the labor and delusional from the medicine, I called out for him. The doors swung open and there stood a man.

"Hello, Kayla Lane?" he asked.

"Yes," I replied with hesitation.

"Mrs. Lane, do you know someone name Carter Lane?"

"Yes, I do and why?" I asked. The man dressed in a police uniform walked closer to my bed as he slowly scanned the room. As he approached me lying there in the bed holding my newborn son, he looked down at us for a second and said, "Is this your son?" He then looked at me and stood there waiting for an answer.

The whole time I am thinking, who else's baby would be lying on my chest after being in labor for hours. Really dude? He just stood there starring at my boy.

"Hmm cute," the officer said. Then he looked at me and introduced himself. "I am Detective Reese." I wondered to myself, detective?

"Well, Detective Reese why are you here?" I asked with a sassy tone in my voice.

"Ok, Mrs. Lane. We received a call tonight from 1527 Winchester Ave," Detective Reese spoke, as he reached into his pocket and pulled out his pen and pad as if he was about to take notes.

"Detective that's my house!"

"Yes, I know. We responded to the call and upon arrival we found the door opened. As we entered the residence, we found suitcases at the door, a car seat full of mail and a small blue knitted blanket. We saw a lot of boxes packed up against the wall. My officers proceeded with caution as they continued searching the residence."

"Ok, you're scaring me detective" I said.

He continued talking, "The officers proceeded to search the kitchen, the den, the dining room, the basement and two out of four of the bedrooms. They waited until I arrived, to go to the other two bedrooms on the third floor. As we reached the third floor there was blood on the wall, then we saw him with pain still in his eyes while clutching a newly opened letter. Would you happened to know anything about a letter Mrs. Lane?"

"No sir, I just know he was supposed to meet me at the hospital."

"I waited for the crime scene unit to arrive, logged in the letter so I could read it. After that was complete, I made a copy, brought it here with me so that you could read it and tell me what this was all about. Oh by the way, congratulations on your new baby." Detective Reese reached in his pocket and passed me the letter.

I trembled with fear, dreading what the letter would say. Slowly, I opened it and began to read.

Dear Kayla,

You are the love of my life and I am so excited about our first child. I wanted you to know that I have been working on a surprise for us and I will be coming to see you on Wednesday at 3:00am so we can talk. I think it is time for us to tell Carter. I know you might not think so but I do, so wait until I tap on the window and then come out. I can't wait to see you. I will be arriving at the Airforce base at 12a.m. then I will be on my way to you.

I Love You,
Jeff

Just then, a single tear fell from my eye.

"Are you ok Mrs. Lane?" Detective Reese inquired.

"Yes, I am."

"Well, I am curious to know who Jeff is?"

"Detective Reese, Jeff is my boyfriend." I lowered my head shamefully.

"I see. Would he have a reason to kill your husband,

Mrs. Lane?" Detective Reese questioned suspiciously.

"No, I don't think so. Well, other than for loving me. Damn, I don't believe this."

I already had told Jeff that it was not his child but he said he always wanted boy and because of his love for me he was willing to do whatever it took to have me and take care of my son. I told him I loved my husband and our family means the world to me. I didn't think he would go to these extremes and I certainly didn't think he would be back from his assignment before Carter and I moved into our new place. I started crying heavily. Why would he kill Carter?

"Oh my God, why?" I screamed, as more tears flowed.

Detective Reese interrupted my train of thought, "Mrs. Lane, I will need you to identify the body and because you are in the hospital I brought a picture. I will leave the folder on this side table so you can look at it after you get yourself together." Detective Reese paused as he reached the door.

"Mrs. Lane, I have police protection outside the door for you. I am going to the cafeteria to get a cup of coffee."

"Ok," I said whimpering to no end. After five minutes past, I had to muster up the energy to look at the folder. It was as if the clock went into stereo, all I could hear was *Tic Toc, Tic Toc, Tic Toc.*

I grabbed the folder and proceeded to open it.

"Oh my God, what the hell? I am confused." Just then, the voice sounded again.

"Hello Kayla."

"What? Who is it?" I said.

"So, you don't know my voice now?"

"Carter?"

"Yes, Kayla."

"Carter? Where are you?" I frantically scanned the room, searching for where his voice was coming from.

"I am right behind you." Carter said as he began to move closer.

"Carter, stop playing!" I yelled, until a hand touched my shoulder and he walked around to the front of me.

"Oh my, Carter! What happened?" I shrieked.

"Hello, Kayla." He kissed me on the forehead and stared at me for a minute.

"What did you do? Carter, what did you do to Jeff?"

"Oh, so you care about your boyfriend huh?" Cater said with an attitude.

"Well, as I was about to leave I kept hearing a tap on the back door window so I walked to the door and jerked it open. I guess I startled him because he sure did jump. Oh yea, earlier today there was a letter that came for you. I decided to open it because I had a funny feeling there was something I needed to know. What a surprise I found, another man in love with my wife." Carter paused and chuckled disturbingly.

"I invited him in the house. I told him you were in the shower and that I was your brother. Then, I confronted him. I asked him about the letter and then I told him to keep it because you were not going to need it. I turned around to open the door, to tell him to leave and he pulled out a knife. When he started to run towards me, I pushed him to the wall and he stabbed himself and bled to death. I am at a lost, this can't be happening. We are supposed to be starting a new life with our new house and new baby, I can't believe this. Kayla I have to go I will be back."

As Carter walked out of the door, I began to cry. Detective Reese came in.

"Mrs. Lane, are you ready to identify the body? I will take your statement." I was getting ready to respond, when Detective Reese received a phone call on his cell. He gestured for me to hold on a second.

"Hello? Yes, ok. I see, alright thank you. I will be there. Good bye." He looked at me with concern in his eyes.

"It seems as if there two bodies found, one in the bedroom and another in the closet. It looks as if the other person was cut with a knife on the arm but it was a major artery. Apparently, he bled out within three minutes; more than enough time for him to walk into the closet.

SILENCE PLAQUED MY ROOM, A DEAD SILENCE....

SUPERSITIONS
By Jodie Pierce

As she stood in the store comparing costumes and prices, a cold and thin male hand reached forward; grabbing her by the shoulder. His face was next to hers and the coldness from his skin radiated off him and onto her. She suddenly had the chills.

"The Victorian dress would look the best on you with your bone structure and posture" he whispered into her ear almost sensually.

She took a step forward and turned around to face the man who thought he knew what was best for her, without even knowing her. She came face to face with a gorgeously thin, tall but pale man with medium length black hair and ice blue eyes. He was dressed in all black except for his name tag.

"He is very sexy" she thought to herself, however she was steaming mad.

"Just who do you think you are?" Trinity asked as the blood started to rise from her neck to her face.

"Oh. Let me introduce myself. I'm Jason and I work here in the Costume/Holiday Department" he said smiling to himself, his hands clasped behind his back. She took a deep breath and started to calm down.

"I saw you debating over the two costumes so I thought

I'd give you my expert opinion" he smiled again.

"Expert?!" she hissed. "Expert, in this rinky dink little store of yours? Do you like to scare all of your customers like that?" she demanded.

"I'm sorry, I didn't mean to-" he said but she cut him off with a wave of her hand. She threw down both costumes and stormed out of the store, jumped into her car and drove off in a huff. He was left standing there dumbfounded. He took off his name tag, stuck it in his pocket and snuck out the back like he'd come in. She'd be back. He was sure of it.

****

All day at work she had been reminded that they were having a Halloween Party in just over two weeks. They basically told everybody that they are expected to have a costume and participate. This depressed Trinity. This time of year really got to her, with all of her Halloween superstitions and it being her birthday. No one at work knew it was her birthday and that's just the way she wanted it.

It was going to be her thirtieth birthday and all she wanted was the routine quiet dinner at her parents' house, followed by her paranoia which lead her to go home; light her candles, do her rituals and go to bed. She had no reason to believe this Halloween was going to be any different but he had different plans for her.

It was Friday and she got paid that day so she decided to attempt to go costume shopping again, nothing had gone right all day for her but she'd try. She went to Halloween USA this time which is a store all about Halloween and only opens around Halloween. She looked for the costume Jason had suggested for in truth, that was the one she preferred but she couldn't tell him that. She looked but they didn't have it in her size which was a very common size for adults. She found two other options but she couldn't find her size in those as well. She began to get frustrated and decided to go back to the original store but just hoped he wouldn't be there to see her swallow her pride.

As soon as she walked back to the costume section, there he stood, holding her costume in the size she needed. She snatched it from him.

"Ok, so you were right" she said trying not to sound too hateful.

"Well, thank you Miss. I love a gal who can admit her mistake" he said smiling. His pearly whites shone through, dazzling her and holding her in a moment of amazement.

"Yeah. Well, I have to go. Thank you for your help" Trinity said, scooping up all her stuff.

"You're welcome" Jason replied as he watched her look and feel ruffled around him. It was exactly what he was going for.

As she got up to the counter, she mistakenly dropped everything including her purse. It was strewn out all across the floor. He flew up from the back to help her pick it up and put it back together.

"Thank you. It's just my dumb luck" she insisted.

"Well, it is Friday the 13th so I'm not surprised. We've had all kinds of things happen to customers today" he consoled her. Jason put the last item back into her purse and she grabbed his hand as he went to pull it out of the purse.

He stopped and looked at her hand, her touch was so warm to him. She looked down as well, but because his hand was so cold on her skin.

"Will you let me thank you and come to dinner at my house tomorrow?" she asked and released his hand. He was taken aback for this was not how he had planned it. He thought it was going to be much harder to get into her house.

"Please? I insist. I'll cook which I do very well" she said

and started writing her address and phone number on a piece of paper and handed it to him. "7pm sharp!" she chimed, as she walked out of the store; forgetting her costume.

****

The following evening, with costume in hand and at 7pm sharp he was standing outside, ringing her doorbell. She had dressed up for the occasion, in a long, black figure hugging dress. The dress was styled with slits up both sides, starting from just above the knees down to the bottom of the dress. He saw her through the doo and she was in her bare feet but her hair and makeup had looked like a professional had done it.

"Nothing like what she usually wore for work" he thought to himself. She was so stunning to him that he felt a little coal of warmth burning within his belly, something he'd never experienced before.

When she opened the door, he was standing there, looking very sexy with a bouquet of flowers in one hand and her costume in other. She checked out his black tailored pants, with a purple dress shirt and a black and grey pin-striped suit vest. He looked amazing as his curls bounced around his face with his every movement. He took off his black leather trench coat and handed it to her. She hung it up for him, though it was almost too heavy for her to lift.

"Can I just say that I am a bozo'?" Trinity asked. "I can't believe after all that, I ended up leaving the costume there. Please let me pay you for it" she insisted.

"Nope. It was left for me to buy it for you and it was fate for me to come over here today" he responded. They smiled at each other until she stuck her nose in the air, excused herself and returned to the kitchen.

"Make yourself at home" she yelled from the other

room.

"I'm a bit nosey so I'll stay on the couch" he replied with a hearty chuckle.

"That's fine. I have nothing to hide" she yelled back.

'Oh really' he said to himself as he got up and went over to her DVD collection.

Interview with the Vampire, Queen of the Damned, John Carpenters Vampires, From Dusk Till Dawn, Daybreakers, Lost Boys and then TV box sets, Moonlight, Kindred: The Embraced, The Vampire Diaries, Dark Shadows-the complete series, True Blood and many more.

"Looks like our little angel has a fascination with vampires" he mumbled just as she was coming out of the kitchen with the roast she had prepared and set it on the table.

"What did you say?" she asked, smiling innocently.

"Oh, it just looks like you like vampire stuff is all" Jason said a little embarrassed.

"Yes. It's my guilty pleasure when it comes to TV or movies" It was her turn for embarrassment.

He helped her into her chair before he took his. Just as she took the salt shaker she dropped it on the floor and it broke. She immediately jumped up, turned around three times in a circle and then threw a pinch of salt over her right shoulder. When she was done, she stopped to look at Jason who was looking on with her almost horrified.

"What was all that about?" he asked, the surprise still in his voice.

"It's a superstition and since superstitions are doubly trouble during Halloween, you have to be careful and take care of them. I could have died if I hadn't done the circle and thrown it over my shoulder" she said solemnly.

Jason was amazed at her belief in these things. It had been so long since he'd met anyone this serious about the superstitions. "I even carry a handkerchief tied in a knot in my purse to ward off evil spirits" she said.

"I saw that when I was helping you pick up your things at the store" he said beginning to see how his plan had just been made easier.

"I'm sorry. I just get weirded out by Halloween, that's all. Most people like it but I just detest it and my birthdays near it so it makes it worse..." she trailed off.

"Whoa!" he said. "Your birthday is on Halloween?" he asked.

"Then you are supposed to be able to see and talk to spirits according to superstition" he said trying to pull her in by seemingly understanding the superstitions.

"Well, I was born on October 30 at 11:58pm which isn't close enough because I've never seen or heard from any spirits. It'd probably freak me out if I did," she said nearly in a panic attack.

He reached his arms out for her to come curl up in his lap. She hesitated at first but something drew her to him. She slowly moved towards him and sat down on his legs. She pulled herself up into a ball and leaned herself against his chest. He rested his head on top of hers and they sat there calmly for a while. He had a soothing effect on her and though she denied it at first, the longer they sat there, the better she realized she felt. Finally, he cleared his throat and she knew what was coming.

"Well, I better get going. It's getting late" he said fighting every primal urge in this body and pit of his stomach to ravage her body, open her up and drink her blood right then and there. However, he had a plan for her so he'd wait.

"reluctantly" he thought as she kissed him on his way out the door. As he walked down the street, his desire for her grew and grew and he didn't know if he'd be able to control the beast within, the next time he had her alone. After he left, she realized they'd never eaten.

******

Over the next two weeks, Trinity and Jason spoke on the phone and made plans to go out together to celebrate her birthday. It was difficult to convince her to go out since she detested celebrating her birthday but he convinced her since it was such an important one. He had decided that her birthday was the perfect time to put his plan in motion since she'd be emotional and susceptible to his charms. She had actually started looking forward to it for she had never had anyone special to celebrate it with.

The day finally arrived. Jason picked up Trinity from her house and on their way back to his car, a black cat ran across their paths. Trinity jumped into Jason's' arms in a hysterical fit.

"Someone's going to die now. I saw the black cat!" she pointed to where the cat had been.

"It's ok Trinity. You are with me and I won't let anything happen to you" he said consoling.

After much comforting, he got her into the car and they went to a nice restaurant for dinner. Trinity noticed again that he didn't eat, he kinda pushed food around on his plate and when he'd been at her house he never ate the roast.

'What's wrong with him?' she wondered to herself. 'He was a picky eater' she told herself in the back of her mind. On the way home, Jason purposely drove past the town cemetery and Trinity started to freak out.

"Oh my gosh. Oh my gosh" she said before sucking in a deep breath and holding it until they completely passed the entire cemetery.

"What's wrong my dear?" Jason asked innocently enough to her but deep down his plan was working.

"It was a cemetery. You have to hold your breath while passing one or the evil spirits can enter your body with your air" she explained.

"Interesting" he said, already knowing the answer to the question before he'd asked it. He'd gone online and looked up "Halloween superstitions" and was given a whole list of them so he was making sure many of them were coming true for Trinity so she would be upset and frail so what he had to do and tell her would be much easier in her condition.

When they got home he purposely parked further away on the street from her house so they had to walk. While walking they were the only ones around but heard footsteps behind them. Jason started to turn around and in a panic. Trinity grabbed him and made him keep walking forward.

"If you hear footsteps behind you, don't look because it could be death coming for you" she explained solemnly. Jason was amused at all her silly superstitions but they endeared her to him. He had started all this as her being his next victim but it turned out to be so much more. He had actually fallen in love with her so the plan had to change. He just hoped it didn't backfire.

As soon as they got in the house, Trinity lit the Halloween candles and walked through each room in the house ringing a small bell. 'The bell scares the evil spirits' she told Jason. Jason eventually got her to sit down on the couch next to him, facing him with her hands in his and looking into his eyes with those big brown chocolate eyes of hers.

"I wanted to talk to you" he said.

"Oh no. Are you breaking up with me?" she asked sadly.

"No no. It's nothing like that" he reassured her.

"Good 'cause that's the last thing I want" she said leaning up kissing him on the lips. He leaned into her to kiss her again, deeper this time and he found his arms embracing her tiny body.

"I have to..." he tried to get out between kisses.

"Yes baby?" she teased him.

"I don't want to lose control...but" he trailed off.

"But what? Lose control Jason. Ravage my body. Hold me tightly and kiss me all over" she encouraged him.

That was all he needed to hear and he started to do exactly as she requested. He kissed her luscious lips, ran his tongue along the tip of her ear from top to bottom and gently wiggled it into the opening while breathing his hot breath on it. He turned her to the side, pulled up the back of her hair and started kissing the back of her neck and playing with the little hairs there which sent shivers down her back. He moved back down to the side of her neck and she took a deep breath in and that was his cue. He couldn't resist any longer. The beast inside him was ready to come out. Just as he bit down into her neck a small squeal of delight came out of Trinity.

"Oh Baby! That is so awesome!" she cooed as he drained her blood. When he stopped, he came up to look at her and still had a trickle of blood running down the side of his mouth. When she saw it she jumped up off the couch and away from him.

"Is that blood?" she asked though she knew the answer.

"Yes my love" he said standing up and moving towards her with his arms outstretched for an embrace. "You have literally two minutes to decide if you want to join me or if all your silly superstitions are going to come true and you will die" he said very calmly, still moving towards her.

"How could you not tell me you're a vampire?" she demanded.

"You never asked" he joked.

"This is not a joking matter. This is life and death" Trinity huffed becoming more and more angry.

"I know. You are so worried about your little superstitions that you haven't learned to live. It's after midnight so you could be born a vampire on Halloween and put all those silly things to rest since as a vampire you are immortal and will never die. This is a gift I am offering you...immortality and to be with me" he explained.

"I have always had a fascination with vampires" she said.

"I know. I saw your DVD collection and figured as much" he said. He looked to her with loving eyes and held out his hand invitingly, waiting for her to come to him. After a brief second, she flew to him and put her head on his chest and he enveloped his arms around her. He bit again back into her neck, giving her that instant feeling of release and pleasure as he drank from her. He then laid her on her back.

"This won't hurt a bit. Just keep drinking until I tell you to stop and keep your eyes closed" he said, as he slit his wrist and put it to her mouth. The blood danced a high paced samba on her tongue and it put her in a euphoric state of mind where everything was peaceful, calm and beautiful.

"Ok, you may now open your eyes and see as a new vampire would" he said encouragingly. Trinity delicately opened her eyes and everything around her was more vibrant and in greater detail. Her eyes made all things beautiful, especially her new companion.

"I'm glad you're here with me" she said, reaching for his hand and holding it inside hers and up to her lips for a gentle kiss.

"I'm just glad I didn't make you my meal!" he said and she gently punched him in the stomach with a smile.

Jodie Pierce: Author of The Vampire Queen trilogy
Please visit my website for more information:
http://www.thevampirequeen1.weebly.com
http://www.thevampirequeen1.wordpress.com
http://www.jodiepierceauthor.blogspot.com
http://www.thevampirequeen1.blogspot.com
http://www.vampiricallyrical.blogspot.com
http://www.amazon.com/author/jodiepierce
http://www.facebook.com/jodie.pierce779
https://www.facebook.com/VampiricalLyrical
http://www.goodreads.com/user/show/5216941-jodie-pierce

KARMA IS A BAD BITCH
By Candii

"Honey, I don't know how to tell you this but we have to stop seeing each other."

"Why Kendrick we have been seeing each other for over a year?"

"Yeah but I never told you this but I'm, well I'm married. My wife knows about us."

"Your who? Kendrick, you are what?" Honey stammered on her words in disbelief.

"Yeah Honey, I'm married and I have two kids with a baby on the way. I'm sorry I never mentioned this."

"Hell no, Kendrick you told me you loved me and that we would get married."

"Honey, I'm sorry baby. We were going through some problems and you were my outlet."

"A fucking outlet? Ken get the fuck out my house." Honey screamed, violently shaking.

"I care about you a lot and I'm sorry to end things this way. My wife is going to divorce me if we continue to sleep around. I will lose everything. My reputation and career could be at stake."

"So, you expect me to be cool with the fact that you are married and have a family. You promised me that we would be together. You're a fucking liar. Ken get the fuck out my house!" Honey yelled, as she tossed the vase full of roses he'd given her earlier that evening.

Ken quickly grabbed his keys and hat, nearly running outside to his car. Honey slammed and locked the house. Stumbling onto the couch, Honey began to cry. She cried so much, that she had given herself a headache and fell asleep. Three hours later she woke up, her eyes were bloodshot and swollen. Snatching her vibrating phone off of the coffee table, she felt the tears welling up in her eyes again. She had two missed calls and three texts from Ken.

9:08PM - *"Honey, I know you are mad with me. I never wanted to hurt you. I care about you greatly. I hope you can forgive me. I don't want you to hate me. I want to remains friends and who knows once my wife thinks things have died down, we may be together again.*

10:08PM – *"Honey, you mean a lot to me and I'm so sorry. I'm hurting just knowing how much I hurt you."*

10:45PM – *"Honey, please text me back"*

Disgusted, Honey threw her phone onto the couch and got up to take a shower.

"I'm going to fix him. Here he is, feeding me lies and false promises all the while he is married. I can't believe this shit." Honey mumbled to herself as she forced herself into the shower.

As the hot water beams against her body, she could no longer hold back her tears.

"I've got to fix his lying ass!" She yelled, as she banged her fist on the ceramic wall tile.

Standing in the shower, head against the wall until the hot water ran out and the pipes started pumping out cold water; Honey stepped out and dried herself off. She threw on some clothes and pulled her hair back into a messy ponytail.

Retrieving her phone from the couch, she hit the sped dial number for her best friend, Valerie.

"Valerie, I need you to come over here. And, make it quick."

"What's wrong Honey? Are you okay?"

"We'll talk when you get here."

"Ok, I'm on the way." Ten minutes later Valerie arrived at Honey's house.

"Girl, you look awful. What's going on?" her friend inquired.

"Val, Ken left me. He came over tonight and told me he is married, that he has a family and that we can't continue to see each other."

"What, Oh my! I'm so sorry for you, Honey." Valerie reached over and hugged Honey tight.

"Time heals all wounds, baby girl. I am here for whatever you need." Valerie spoke, as she consoled her longtime friend.

Valerie and Honey had always been more like sisters than they were friends. After knowing each other for over ten years, and always being each other's support system; blood couldn't make them any closer. When one was affected by something, the other was always right there.

Valerie glanced down at her watch, "Damn, is it that late already?"

"I am sorry, girl. I know it's late and you have to be at work early tomorrow. I just needed to vent and let some steam off my chest.

"No, it's okay. You said you needed me, so I am here. I thought ahead and brought my work clothes with me."

"You're the best, Val." Honey smiled weakly as she laid her head in Valerie's lap. It wasn't long before both women dozed off.

Two weeks have gone by and Ken hasn't slowed down with his persistence. Every day, he emailed, called, and texted Honey. Honey was still hurting by his bombshell. She couldn't gather the strength nor the courage to reply to him. She was still trying to figure out her plan of revenge and couldn't risk speaking to him and he win her over. To help distract her mind, Honey started taking overtime shifts with the hopes it would help get her mind off of being lonely at home.

One afternoon, while in the breakroom making copies of files; Honey began to feel lightheaded and slightly dizzy. Grabbing the closest chair, she took a seat and tried to wait for the feeling to subside. A strong sense of urgency came over Honey and overwhelmed her with a need to vomit. Weakly walking to the ladies' room, she stumbled into the stall. Five minutes later and a lunch lighter, Honey felt a little better. Not wanting to think too much into it, she blamed her sudden illness on the stress from the breakup.

Not feeling up to staying at work, Honey called Valerie to pick her up.

As soon as Valerie saw her friend, she knew something wasn't right.

"You look so flushed, Honey. Where do want me to take you. Home or to the doctor?"

"Val, please take me home. I hope I'm not coming down with the flu or something."

Valerie did as her friend asked, even though she didn't agree. When they got to Honey's house, Valerie made a cup of chamomile tea for Honey to sip on. After finishing the cup, Honey fell asleep. It wasn't even a half hour later, before Honey popped up covering her mouth and made a run for the bathroom.

Standing at the doorway, Valerie had seen enough.

"Honey, I am taking you to see doctor. Get showered and dressed, I'll be waiting in the livingroom."

An hour later, the two ladies sat in the slightly crowed urgent care office; waiting for Honey to be called. As soon as Honey was finished filling out the registration, she was called into the triage area. After answering some routine questions, the nurse took Honey's vitals and handed her a plastic container for a urine sample.

After what felt like an eternity, Honey was called into the back and set up in one of the private rooms. As she got herself comfortable on the table, in walked the doctor.

"Congratulations, Ms. Honey. You are six weeks pregnant."

A speechless and emotional Honey stared at the doctor in disbelief.

"I am pregnant? Are you sure?" she questioned.

"Indeed, I am. But, I'll do a quick ultrasound just to be sure."

Laying Honey back, the doctor covered the lower half of her body and slowly entered the probe into her. Locating the embryo almost instantly, the doctor pointed to the screen.

"See, that there is your little growing person."

Honey's mouth dropped at the sight of her baby. She was actually carrying another person in her womb; small tears fell from her eyes.

"Now, you will need to follow up with an ob/gyn clinic or physician but here's a prescription for prenatal vitamins. Do you have any questions?"

Honey sat with her mouth agape, shaking her head as he handed her the script, still in shock.

When she reaches the waiting room, Valerie looks up with a look of concern on her face. "Everything good boo?"

"No Val, but we'll talk in the car," Honey insisted, not wanting to break down again in front of everyone in the waiting room.

In the car, Honey tells Val she's pregnant. Valerie tries to console her and but she is speechless. "Let me get you home and we can try to figure this out."

"Val, he has a wife and a child on the way. There is no way that I'm keeping this baby."

"Honey, I know that you are deeply hurt and this is so unexpected. But first, I think you should tell him and talk things over. Whatever you decide, you know that I have your back, but you need to weigh your pros and cons."

"You're right," Honey agreed. "I'll call him as soon as I get back to the house. Will you stay with me?"

"Of course, I will. There ain't no way I'm leaving you by yourself."

The drive back to Honey's house was silent. Honey wondered how Ken would react to hearing that she was carrying his child. Thoughts of him leaving his wife and coming to be a family with her, gave her a false sense of hope and made her excited to talk with him. As soon as she got home, she dialed his number. He answered on the third ring.

"Hello, Honey" Ken excitedly answered.

"Hello, Ken. We need to talk."

"Yes, we do Honey. I've missed you. How have you been?"

"Ken, cut the small talk. I've only called to tell you that I'm pregnant."

"Don't play with things like that Honey, I know I hurt you and all but don't play."

His non sense of urgency or excitement, pissed Honey off and busted any visions she'd had of them maybe being a family.

"Don't play? Ken, why the fuck would I lie? I went to the doctor today and I have the confirmation. I hate you, I really do! You better tell your wife before I do. You have thirty days or I'll help you out." Honey spat.

There was a brief silence on the other end. "Honey, tomorrow I will wire you a thousand dollars to get rid of it."

Slamming the phone down, she hung up before she could say something that she would regret later on. Distraught, disgusted and feeling disrespected; Honey asked Valerie to leave so that she may have some space to think. Valerie was hesitant but she respected her friend's wishes with the promise that Honey would call her later on. As she watched Valerie pull out of her driveway, only one thing flooded Honey's mind; revenge.

Taking a seat on her couch, Honey decided to call up her brother, Wesley; who so happens to be a police officer.

"What's up, Sis" Wesley answered.

"Nothing much, bro. I need a favor though"

"Anything." Wesley replied, hearing the pain in his sister's voice.

Honey gave him the names of Kendrick and his wife and asked for him to do a little digging. Twenty minutes later, Wesley called back with full report on home and work address, the car they drive, and more. Excited, Honey thanked her brother and promised to visit him and her nieces soon before ending the call. That was more than enough information for Honey to use.

With her wheels of revenge turning in motion, Honey looks up his wife on Facebook. Instantly sickened, Honey scrolled through her page. It was plastered with pictures of Ken, her and their kids; looking like one big happy family. Only if he knew what was coming to him, Honey was going to make him pay for all the pain he'd caused her.

The next twenty-nine days went by quickly. Honey had been on the countdown ever since her last conversation with Ken. He'd been avoiding her since she told him that she was pregnant. The last message she received from him was that informing her of the wire he made for her to terminate the pregnancy. Honey checked her phone, still no messages from Ken. She decided to send short and simple email, reminding him that tomorrow would be the day she told his wife. After hitting send, Honey signed into Facebook and searched his wife's page. She closed out the page after only a few minutes, it truly hurt to see pictures of his children, wife, and her growing baby bump.

****

By two o'clock the next day, she still hadn't heard from Ken. Not being able to deal with the feeling of abandonment from him, Honey had enough. It was time for him to feel a fraction of the pain he'd caused her. She grabbed her notebook with the wife's number and decided to call her.

"Hello." Camille answered the private number.

"Hi, Camille. My name is Honey but I am sure you know this already. As you know, Ken and I have been in relationship for a whole year. During that time, I knew nothing about you. He sprung the news on me about two and half months ago. But that is neither here nor there, the reason behind my call today is to inform you that I'm also pregnant with his baby. I'm sure he didn't tell you this."

"Bitch you're lying! You only wish that you were having his baby. You are nothing more than a homewrecker and a slut." Camille spat.

"Ok, Camille if that's how you want to play it. I am going to expose both you and your husband. Next time, don't be such a low self-esteemed wife. You knew he was cheating yet you gave him an ultimatum. But, watch this bitch. This is not over." Honey ended the call.

The next day, Honey received an email from Ken.

Honey,

I sent you the money a few weeks ago. Please Honey, use it to get rid of it. I'm sorry this happened but I have to cut all ties. Honey, my family and career is on the line and I can't afford for this kind of drama to ruin my reputation.

Ken

That email was the straw that broke the camel's back.

Honey was furious and could not fathom the thought of her love leaving her, being married and having a family. And, to add insult to injury; wanting her to kill their unborn child. It was game time, and she was ready to play. She gathered all the evidence she had; sonograms, photos, text messages, and emails. She even included a video of them having sex. Once she had all that she needed, she sent a nice lengthy email with the attachments to Ken's boss and all of off his superiors; informing them of the lying cheating scum he really was.

Even though she was sure she'd just cost him his job, she still wasn't satisfied. She called his wife's job and let the recording of her and Ken having sex, play on the company's voicemail. Honey was on a mission; all she saw was red. Continuing on her warpath of destruction, Honey created a fake Facebook page. She started posting messages on his wife's post about their affair, and even started tagging her in photos of them together.

Hours passed, and she hadn't heard a thing. Finally, Honey decided to change her phone number and close her email accounts. She really didn't feel like hearing from Ken or his wife. She simply wanted them to feel embarrassed and hurt the way she felt when she found out about everything.

******

Kendrick didn't know what to expect when his boss called him in for an emergency meeting. What happened next, was his worst nightmare come true. In the meeting, Ken was brought up to speed and made painfully aware of the lengths a woman scorned would go to, as he watched an intimate session with Honey being displayed in front of the highest members within the company.

"This type of behavior, Kendrick is not acceptable. And, because of your position and title within the company;

we have decided that you need to resign." Ken's head superior spoke.

Just like that, twelve years of hard work and being the company's CEO and spokesperson; gone within a matter of minutes. Kendrick gathered his personal items from what used to be his office and did the walk of shame with his head hung low, to the elevator. Once he reached his car, he attempted to call his wife but she didn't answer.

"Honey!" He screamed as he jumped into his car and peeled off, in route to Honey's house.

When he arrived, Honey wasn't there. While waiting out front, he tried calling her cellphone. An automated operator blared through the phone. "The number that you dialed, is no longer in service."

"Shit." Ken's heart began to race as he hurries home. He says a silent prayer, asking that he at least be able to speak to his wife and beg for forgiveness.

****

As soon as Camille went into work, she was reprimanded because of the voicemail. Her director urged her to keep the drama at home and not in the workplace, after placing her on a week's suspension for the incident and sending her home. Camille was humiliated and ashamed, being nine months pregnant and now all of her co-workers knew was having trouble in her marriage. The drive home, Camille was an emotional wreck. She tried calling Honey, but to no avail. Distraught, Camille calmly waited for her husband to return home.

When Kendrick pulled up in front of his house and saw Camille's car in the driveway; he sat outside for a few minutes as he gathered his composure. A lump formed in his throat, as he inserted his key and opened the door. The house was unusually quiet.

"Camille, baby we need to talk." Ken called out as he

walked slowly into the foyer.

"There is nothing left to talk about, Ken. You've embarrassed me for the last time." Camille pulled out a .38 and aimed it at Ken's head.

Without a second thought, Camille let off a single round; dropping Ken where he stood. She quickly put the gun in her purse and used her gloved hands to ransack the house. Pulling the gun from her purse, she ran around the back of the house and used the butt of the gun to shatter the small window near the back door. Running back around, she left the front door slightly ajar.

Calmly, she wipes the gun clean, places it in a handkerchief and back into her purse. She drives over to the daycare center and picks up her children. On the way home, she stopped by McDonald's and ordered the children happy meals. Before pulling off, she emptied one of the McDonald's bags and placed the gun inside; tossing the bag inside the dumpster located behind the restaurant.

When she arrived home, she pretended to discover Kendrick's dead body. Immediately, she calls the police in a horrified state about her discovery. Upon arrival, the detectives get a statement from her and inform her that her husband appeared to have been murdered during a home invasion gone wrong. A week later, Camille went into labor and gave birth to a healthy baby girl. When she was released, she took her $450,000.00 life insurance check from Ken's death and packed up her and her children; relocating to Phoenix with her mother and father.

****

As the months passed since Ken's untimely demise, Honey's pregnancy furthered. Honey moved in with Valerie after learning of Ken's murder. She was having a hard time adjusting, so Valerie suggested that she seek counseling to help her cope with the stresses of her unplanned pregnancy and the permanent loss of Ken. Honey felt like she was the cause of Ken's death, and it weighed heavy on her conscious.

At six and half months, Honey's body went in early labor. After an emergency cesarean, she gave birth to two-pound baby boy; that she named Kendrick Jr. KJ was placed in the NICU, immediately as he fought for his life. A week later, the doctors regretfully inform Honey that KJ didn't make it.

The stress of losing another person she loved, was too much to bare. Honey suffered a severe mental breakdown and was admitted into a mental institution. Valerie stood by her friend and visited as often as she could.

In a few short months, the lives of Kendrick, Camille, Honey, and her unborn baby changed for the worst. Karma is a bad bitch and what goes around comes around.

THE FIRST SHALL BE LAST
By King Diamond

PART ONE

"Mother, please sign the papers. I know you that you don't want me to do it, but what other choices do we have? I'm tired of seeing you suffer like this, trying to raise us and support us all by yourself," he pleaded again, fed up with watching his mother cry and struggle to provide for their family.

The country was engaged in a very taxing war, and the military was desperately seeking new recruits. Roderick had just turned seventeen but the required age for enlistment was eighteen, which meant that his mother would have to lie about his age in order for him to be accepted. If she didn't, he was prepared to forge her signature on the application himself. Not that he wanted to, but it was a sacrifice that he was prepared to make for their family.

Nancy looked at her eldest son with misty eyes. It wasn't lying that was eating away at her heart; it was the realization that if she complied that it could very well be the last time that she would ever lay eyes upon her son again. Every day on the news, she watched in dismay as thousands of military soldiers lost their lives in a war that she really felt made no sense whatsoever. Having her son possibly added to that list was just something that she wouldn't be able to cope with.

"Maybe when I get this other job at the warehouse things will get better Monkey. Plus, your father's supposed to be coming home from off of the fishing boat in a couple more weeks. Why don't we just wait until then, and if things aren't going well then I will sign the papers," she told him, trying to find a reasonable way to placate her son.

Roderick wasn't about to back down from his decision. He loved and respected his mother with all of his heart, yet he knew that she was just trying to buy a little more time. The bills were overdue, the food was so scarce that they were drinking sugar water and eating mayonnaise sandwiches, their clothes and shoes were being supplied through the Salvation Army; so many problems without a realistic, foreseeable answer to them in the near future.

"Okay mother, we can do that. I just want us all to be able to live a decent life," he agreed, yet only to put her mind at ease.

"Thank you baby, now go and help your sister Gail with her homework while I fix dinner. Mister Paul gave us some fish and shrimps that he caught yesterday at the creek," she told him, giving him the best reassuring smile that she could.

When Nancy came home the next day from work her daughter Tammy met her at the door with a folded up piece of paper clutched inside of his hand. She thought that it was probably something from his school. She unfolded it and almost had a heart attack, the tears brimming up inside of her eyes immediately as she saw that it was from her son Roderick.

Dear Mother,

I know that when you get this letter, you'll probably be upset. But, you have done your best to take care of us and now it's time for me to do mine. I'm sorry for forging your signature but I had no choice, and I hope that you forgive me. Also, I hope that you forgive me for lying to you about waiting until we see what happens in two weeks.

They said that we will be home in no less than four years, so I will send you my check each week to take care of the family. Pray for me and I promise to keep in touch. I love you so much mother, that's why I just couldn't sit by and watch our family go through this any longer. When my father gets home please explain it to him.

I'm on my way to some place in Carolina called Fort Bragg. As soon as I get a chance to call you or write again I will. My girlfriend Pamela knows what I've done and she understands, and I hope that I have your blessings on this journey too.

Love you always,
Roderick

PART TWO

"Jerome Cohen, report to the visitation area, you have a visit!" the CO's voice blared out into the dormitory from the intercom speakers.

Without a second's hesitation, he threw his cards on the table and stood. There were only two things right now that could make him move that fast; his visits and when mealtime was announced.

"Boo Brown, take over that hand for me. I've got a really good one this time," he told one of the inmates who'd be standing around watching the card game. He excused himself, making a beeline for the officer's station to be let out of the dormitory for visitation. Every Saturday, for the past two years, his wife and his daughter had made the two-hour trip to Bakerstown Correctional Institution to show their unconditional love and support.

Jerome had been sentenced to a three-year prison term for a crime that he honestly didn't commit. He'd purchased a gun from a crackhead out of the neighborhood, only to discover that it'd been used in a convenient store robbery. To make matters worse, he resembled the actual person that'd committed the crime and had no alibi as to his whereabouts that day. The supposed-to-be jury of his peers that were not only racist but from a different class, wasted no time in reaching a guilty verdict.

"Name?" the CO standing outside of the back door to the visitation area with the clipboard asked him.

"Jerome Cohen sir," he told him.

The CO found his name on the clipboard and checked it off, opening the door and stepping aside to allow him entrance. He crossed the threshold into the dimly lit room, where two of his fellow inmates were getting dressed again to go into the main section.

"Okay Cohen, you know the drill," a CO who knew him instructed, putting on a fresh pair of latex gloves.

Without a slight hesitation, he began to get undressed. Once done, the CO did a visual inspection to make sure that he wasn't trying to introduce any illegal contraband into the visitation area. He then checked his clothing, handing them back to him once he'd satisfied his curiosity.

"It's almost over isn't it Cohen?" the CO asked as he was getting dressed.

"Yes sir, four more months," he responded, anxiously awaiting the day.

Once dressed, he opened the door that led into the main area of the visitation building, at once spotting his wife Lacadiette and their daughter Angel. The distance between them seemed to close faster than the Red Sea, after it had parted to let the people of Egypt pass through and drown Pharoah.

Not one single word was voiced as tears of joy fell, smiles lit up, and the loving embrace of the familial trio blotted out the entire world around them. Afterwards, they walked back over to the table that Lacadiette had reserved for them and sat down.

"Roderick said to tell you that he already has a job set up for you at the shipyard," she told him.

"Tell him I said thanks baby. So how's Ronnie doing?" he asked, referring to his eighteen-year old son.

"Trying to run the house and tell everybody what to do," his daughter cut in, drawing laughter from the both of them.

"He's doing okay baby. He is really hyped about his graduation next month," his wife told him.

"I sure wish I could be there to see him walk across that stage baby," he responded, knowing that his son looked up to him and would really want him to be there to share in the huge accomplishment.

What neither of them knew though was that he'd been in the education program himself for the last six months, and in three months he'd be taking the test to earn his GED. When his father had come back from the military he and his mother had gotten married. Sadly, they hadn't lasted two years before they'd divorced and went their separate ways. His mother's desire to place her male flings before her own child caused him to deviate from the right path, and at the age of fourteen he was expelled from school.

"So, how're things going at the hair salon baby? I hear that y'all are doing big things these days," he told her, grinning.

"It's going great baby. We're starting to get more exposure than ever before," she told him, smiling.

"That's good baby," he replied, before turning his attention to his daughter.

"And what about you there, mam? What's been going on in the life of the little Miss Diva herself," he kidded, chuckling.

Angel took her manicured small hand and brushed back a bang of her long, silky hair from her face, flashing her father with a pearly white smile.

"Well, since you did respect my status let me give you the latest update dad. I have a 4.0 GPA, I've been selected to enter a college preparatory program next year at JU, and I'm scheduled to do two photoshoots next week," she listed, proud of what she was accomplishing thus far.

"Oh wow, congratulations Miss, and keep up the good work," he complimented her, always thankful that his children were focused and positively driven in life.

For the next few hours they all basked in the joy of the visit, chatting, joking, laughing, and treating themselves to some of the edible treats that the canteen offered. As always, when the CO announced that visitation was ending the reality set in. Though the once-a-week opportunity was a sufficient Band-Aid to get them through another six lonely days, realizing that they would be returning home and that he wouldn't always shredded their hearts.

"Okay now ladies, don't make me cry up in here in front of all of these folks. If these other inmates see it they might think I'm soft, and then my name going to be Jeronicka instead of Jerome by the time I come home," he joked, causing both of them to crack up with laughter.

PART THREE

Ronnie saw the mailman coming up the street as he was engaged in a fact finding debate with his next door neighbor Hassan. They'd soon become friends ten years ago when the Muslim youth and his family had moved there. At first, Ronnie was just as wary of them as the other people in the neighborhood, biasedly stereotyping them as evil terrorists with a crazy religious concept.

"You just hold on to that thought right there for a second buddy. I see a tiny little crack in that theory you just stated," he told him, walking over to the fence to get the mail from the mailman. As he walked back over to Hassan he rifled through it, looking for anything that had his name upon it; No luck today.

"Okay Hassan, now let me get this right. You say that in the Holy Quran it says that Jesus didn't die on the cross?" he asked for the sake of clarification.

"Sure did my friend, and if you read your Bible using your own perception instead of that of someone else then it will be crystal clear to see," he replied.

"I will definitely be doing that as soon as I go inside. In the meantime, if that was true then basically you're telling me that He didn't die for my sins," Ronnie countered, trying to prove the absurdity of Hassan's viewpoint.

"That's exactly what I'm telling you Ronnie, because if He did then what is the need for Judgment Day? Let me ask you a something; If you touch a hot stove do you get burned or is it Jesus that gets burned?" he asked, preparing to give him a better way to look at his viewpoint.

"Don't be ridiculous now Hassan, that's a no brainer," he replied.

"It sure is ridiculous my friend, as is the perception that a person does the sin but Jesus gets the punishment. In this country there's an age old saying that for every action there's a reaction, and yet when it comes to sin y'all think that because Jesus supposedly died on the cross the reaction is salvation," he explained, shaking his head at the ludicrous theory.

Ronnie was just about to reply when he saw the aqua green Lexus pull up at the curb. He excused himself and walked over to meet his girlfriend, rewarding her with a possessive hug and a passionate kiss. Karen was the unbendable axis upon which his world turned. She waved over at Hassan before turning her attention back to the love of her life. Since they'd met in the seventh grade at Eugene. Butler Middle School the two had become inseparable.

"I got a little surprise for you baby," she told him, her face lighting up with a smile.

"I just love surprises baby," he responded, grinning from ear to ear.

Karen reached into her purse and came out with an envelope, handing it to him. She looked on in silent anticipation as he opened it, knowing that he'd be overjoyed to find out the good news.

As Ronnie began to read the letter, his eyes grew wide in shock and his mouth hinged open. Since twelve years old he'd had a passion for reading and writing. As the years went on it became more and more intense, to the point that his mother would find him asleep at the table with his head resting on a book some mornings.

It was a letter from Hoodography Publications, advising him that after reviewing the portion of the novel that he'd submitted they would be contacting him about signing a contract. He'd felt that he wasn't good enough to be on this kind of level, so without his knowledge Karen had been the one to submit the manuscript for him. His eyes misted over as he looked up at her speechless, so filled with joy that all he could do was bring her into his arms in a tight, affectionate embrace.

"Congratulations baby," she whispered into his ear as they held each other, happy that his dream would now soon become a reality.

"Thank you so much baby, for believing in me when I didn't even believe in myself," he told her, truly grateful that God had brought her into his life as a mate.

"Oh no mister, you're not getting off that easy. Thank me with an engagement ring, a few children, a big house, a convertible Benz, a new wardrobe," she ran down the list playfully, counting off each request with a finger.

Ronnie burst forth with gales of laughter, throwing up his hands in surrender.

"Okay-okay-okay baby, you win," he seceded, shaking his head at her always tickling sense of humor. Karen couldn't hold back any longer, her own laughter filling the atmosphere. Other than the engagement ring and the desire to bear his children, nothing else that she'd listed mattered to her. Regardless of how rich or poor that he'd be in life, she loved him for him.

"So how's everybody doing?" she asked once they'd gone into the house.

"My mother and Angel went to visit my father, my brother Michael is at the park, and my brother Herbert is over to his friend's house," he informed, grabbing the remote and cutting on the television.

"So how much longer does your father have in that place? She asked.

"I think somewhere around four months. My mother told me that he tried to apply for the work release program, but because of his charges they denied him," he explained.

"Well I'm just glad that this is all about to be over baby. I know you miss him, and I hope that when he gets out his life can return to normal. When my Uncle Bob got out it was hard for him to get a job or any kind of help, and he ended up going right back," she recalled, determined to become a lawyer so that she can free her favorite uncle.

"That's crazy baby, but my grandfather has a job already lined up for him at the shipyard so he doesn't have to worry about that part. I just hope that he stays away from anything that can get him sent back to prison again. Even though he's in there on a humbug, just associating with the people he knew when he was running the streets is too risky," he told her, finally finding the television station where the Florida Gators football game was just about to begin.

PART FOUR

The long trip back to Jacksonville, Florida seemed like forever, especially since he hadn't told anyone that he'd be coming home. Gone was the muscularly chiseled, military soldier with a finely tapered mustache and goatee, replaced by a pepper headed and bearded, Purple Heart recipient who would forever walk with a limp.

"Man, I can't wait to get home to my mother's home cooked meals. Those C-rations so nasty I bet they have dog food that tastes better than that stuff," a soldier from his hometown who'd enlisted with him voiced from the seat beside him.

"I definitely agree with you on that. Plus, it's been over three years of smelling nothing but sweaty men. I need to smell some of that sweet smelling perfume that my woman wears right about now," he replied, anxiously anticipating that moment of having her in his arms again.

"Well me and my child's mother broke up right before I joined the Army, so I'm going to be enjoying the smell of a few strippers this weekend," he responded, both of them laughing.

The light banter between them went on all the way up until Ronnie decided to take a brief nap, his Army mate agreeing that it was a good idea. The next time he opened his eyes they'd arrived at the Jacksonville International Airport.

"Home sweet home", he thought to himself, a cheesy grin forming upon his face.

PART FIVE

Jerome waited for his wife to accept the collect call charges with a sense of elated pride. Not only would his son be graduating from high school today, but he'd passed his pre-GED test and would be taking the actual one next week. To a lot of the other inmates it was probably just something to pass time, yet it meant the world to him.

"Hey there love of my life, how's your day going?" Lacadiette greeted him cheerily, always trying to stay in high spirits.

"Every day is a good day when you have the best woman in the world as your wife baby," he replied, a declaration that he believed with all of his heart.

"Aw, how sweet baby," she thanked him, sending him a kiss through the phone.

"Where's Ronnie at baby? I want to congratulate him on finishing school and earning his Diploma," he told her, so proud of his son.

Lacadiette took the phone away from her ear and called out to her son that his father was on the phone. He emerged from the hallway making a swift beeline towards his mother. She handed him the phone, heading back into the kitchen to prepare dinner.

"Hey there old timer, how things been going?" he greeted his father kiddingly, both of them chuckling.

"The only thing old about me son is this cigarette habit I have, and I'm about to get rid of that," he assured him.

"That's great. Every time I see one of those anti-smoking commercials I switch channels because I know that I'm going to start thinking about you," he voiced, always praying for the day when his father would quit.

"Well since I'm not going to be able to attend the graduation or give you another kind of gift, I thought that if I gave up smoking that would be something that you might like too. Congratulations Ronnie, I'm so proud of you son," he praised him, smiling because he could imagine the smile on his son's face right now.

"To be honest, I think that's the best gift I ever received in my life," he responded, looking up towards the ceiling and thanking God.

PART SIX

"We now present to you the Class of 2015," the principal of Ribault High School announced through the microphone, the entire audience rising to their feet and applauding the graduates.

Their names were called one by one in alphabetical order to walk up and receive their Diploma. Always known to be the class clown amongst his teachers and fellow classmates, everybody wondered what kind of crazy stunt Ronnie would pull when his name was called. Keeping a straight, officious face, he sat there silently and awaited his name to be called. He was the fifth one on the list, so the wait wasn't long at all.

"Ronnie Cohen!" the principal announced, the crowd erupting into a frenzied applause.

He rose from his seat and continued to keep his poker face intact. He walked up to the principal and received his Diploma, shaking his hand. He turned to the crowd and waved to them, then turned and began to walk back towards his seat. That's when the funny, always clowning Ronnie proceeded to give the crowd a memorable, epic treat.

After about four paces his forward steps suddenly became backwards ones, the 'Moonwalk' maneuver created by Michael Jackson taking the crowd by utter surprise. When he'd moonwalked back to where the principal was standing he halted, spun towards the crowd, and began to do the 'Dougie' dance.

It was a graduation ceremony that nobody present would ever forget.

PART SEVEN

Because he was bored and tired of just sitting around the house, Roderick had decided to return back to school and earn his Diploma. His wife Pamela had told him that he could take his classes online, but for some reason there was a fueled drive inside of him to be amongst the young students. At sixty-one years old he'd most likely be older than his teacher, yet he'd heard of other elderly people who'd done it so it boosted his confidence.

At first, the rowdy, wild students in his twelfth grade class alienated him because of his age. But it didn't take long for his down-to-earth, friendly vibe win them over, his new nickname 'Old School'. Not only was he excelling academically, he'd become sort of a Dr. Phil to those who had issues that they felt uncomfortable addressing their parents with.

The end of the school year was fast approaching, and they were rehearsing for the graduation ceremony.

"Okay y'all, we need someone to do the commencement speech for our graduating class. Any suggestions?" the teacher asked.

Every student in the audience eyes fell upon Roderick, feeling that there wasn't a more deserving person after the brave, courageous act that he'd undertaken by returning to finish school. All he could do was throw up his hands in surrender and grin, too emotionally overwhelmed to even speak. The best part of it all was that he and his wife Pamela had decided that they'd keep it a secret until the day of graduation.

PART EIGHT

Jerome walked through the gates of Bakerstown Correctional Institution with a big smile spread across his face, feeling the euphoric, adrenalized energy like that of a caged animal released back into the wild. His wife Lacadiette and Angel were standing excitedly in the parking lot, ready to get back to Jacksonville and celebrate this long awaited moment.

After hugging and kissing them, they hopped in the rented Astro Van and headed home. During the almost two hour trip they caught up on the past and present, and talked of their plans for the future. It seemed like no time had elapsed at all before they were pulling up to the house, where Ronnie, Michael, Herbert, and a large throng of family and friends had the welcome home festivities in full swing.

"Okay everybody; it's time to turn up for my main man. Welcome home daddy," Michael excitedly yelled out through the microphone, he and a couple of his deejay friends providing the party's music.

To the happy, upbeat sounds of Maze featuring Frankie Beverly's 'Back In Stride Again, Jerome, Lacadiette, and Angel walked up into the crowd, everybody converging upon them to welcome him home. Though he fought hard to hold back the tears that threatened to pour from his eyes, on the inside a torrential downpour was taking place.

"Daddy come on up here and say a few words," Michael called out to him, waving him up to the deejay area.

Jerome tried to decline but everybody egged him on, his wife playfully pulling him up to the microphone. Reluctantly, he accepted it from his son with a grin.

"Now y'all know I don't like to be put on the spot like this, but since I got a surprise for y'all let me get this on out the way," he opened, feeling like this was the perfect timing for his announcement.

He opened the small tote bag that he'd stored all of his property he'd left prison with, and fished around until he found what he was looking for. He grabbed the document and then began to address them all again.

"While I was locked up I made a promise to myself that I was going to change a lot of things in my life, because I realized that I'm not the kind of man that prison was made for. One of those things was to finish a goal that I started a long time ago, and though it may seem like nothing to some people it's priceless to me," he told them, handing his son back the microphone and held up his GED certificate for all to see.

PART NINE

"Baby, I didn't know your mother was teaching school," Lacadiette voiced as they all entered the auditorium's lobby.

"Well I knew she worked at the daycare center, but this looks like a high school graduation ceremony," he responded, baffled also.

"It sure is. This graduation is for Raines High School. They must've made a mistake about the address," Ronnie told them, recognizing a few of the graduates who also lived in their neighborhood.

Karen saw them as soon as they entered and called out to them, waving them over.

"Y'all follow me. I already have some seats reserved for us," she told them, leading the way.

As they came through the door that led into the main section of the auditorium, the principal had already begun to speak.

"I now introduce to you the William M. Raines High School graduating class of 2015," he announced, a thunderous applaud ensuing as the graduates walked single file onto the stage and took their seats.

Simultaneous to them sitting down it was Michael who spotted his grandfather first, pointing excitedly at him walking to his seat in the maroon and grey cap and gown outfit.

"Y'all look. That's granddaddy up there," he bellowed out in shock, all of them following his pointing finger to where Roderick was walking in the line.

"Lord have mercy, I just know that isn't my father up on that stage," Jerome voiced in disbelief, swearing that his mind was playing tricks on him. He turned to his mother who was just sitting there with a huge grin on her face, the others following suit.

Karen threw up her hands and shrugged.

"I didn't have anything to do with it. Your father said he was going back to school, and all I did was support his decision. I couldn't tell anybody because he wanted to keep it a secret. Well, I guess it's not a secret anymore," she told them, smiling.

All of them looked on in wondrous pride as Roderick sat on the stage amongst his graduating class, the eldest of them all. After the principal had announced their names and presented them all with their high school diplomas, it was time for the graduating classes address to the audience.

"I would now like all of you to give a round of applause to our next speaker who will speak on behalf of our graduating class of 2015; Mr. Roderick Cohen," the principal announced, joining in the thunderous applause.

Not only did they applaud as he walked up to the podium, but they all rose in a standing ovation. The entire auditorium lit up with the blinding flash of cameras, everybody eager to capture such a momentous moment. It wasn't every day that a man who'd already reached the senior citizen status made a decision to undertake such an accomplishment, truly inspiring to the elderly people present who'd failed to earn their diploma.

Roderick had tried many times to prepare a speech, but for some reason he just didn't like them when he read over them again. That was the reason why he'd just decided to speak from the heart, hoping that what he said would motivate those who'd dropped out of school to return and complete their goal also.

"When I was seventeen years old I watched my mother and father struggle to raise my brothers and sisters, and I just felt that I had to do something. So when the war broke out and the Army was begging for recruits, against my mother's better judgment I enlisted. I was already in the twelfth grade and really wanted to graduate, but sometimes life calls for you to make some very hard sacrifices. Which is one of the reasons why I'm standing on this stage today, opposed to on the one that I should've been standing on many, many years ago.

"The other reason was fear, and I know that there're probably a few people in the crowd right now who can relate to what I'm admitting right now. When I look back at it now it's funny to me, because to be honest what did I really have to be afraid of? It wasn't like I was going to be sitting in a classroom with aliens from another planet," he joked, turning to look at his classmates with a playful grin on his face.

"Well, I actually did feel like a few of them acted like they were when I first got there," he kidded, chuckling while everybody in the audience laughed.

"Seriously though, I wouldn't trade them or the experience for the world. Throughout the entire year we helped each other to accomplish this mission, but not only that we helped each other to become better individuals. So I guess that old saying that age isn't anything but a number is true this time.

"In closing, I would like to encourage all of you who've been scared to go back to school and get your GED or Diploma to put the fear behind you. It only exists because you allow it to, so stop breathing life in it and finish out your mission," he went on, a few of the elderly people in the crowd teary eyed by the speech. He turned back to his graduating class with a huge, affectionate smile upon his face.

"Thanks for everything y'all, and I really enjoyed our experience. Like that rap guy Drake y'all be listening to say, 'we started from the bottom now we here'," he ended, the entire auditorium erupting into a celebratory frenzy as he bowed and proceeded back to his chair amongst his graduating class.

ALWAYS ON THE WRONG SIDE OF LOVE
By Rasheemah

CHAPTER ONE

My sister always told me my man hating ways would catch up with me but I didn't believe her. I wasn't always like this but it all changed when my first love left me without an explanation. It turned my heart cold against the opposite sex. I didn't believe anything they said or did because to me none of them could be trusted. Whenever they got to close I would find a way to pull away from them or just disappear and never speak to them again.

"Tamika, what's been going on with you? I haven't talked to you in months" Toni asked.

"Girl, so much shit has happened. Are you sure you have enough time to listen the last couple months of my life?" I said.

"Yes girl, I have nothing but time. I'm just happy you called me over here. I missed you so much and I know if mom could see us now she would be happy" she stated.

"Let me get us some drinks and roll something up because once I finish this story you're going to need it" I told her. I got up and prepared everything while she went to the bathroom.

I had to get my thoughts together because what I was about to reveal would be like therapy for me and I needed it badly. So much as happened in to me in the twenty-five years on this earth. I just prayed that God could heal my heart and show me that all love is, not bad love. Toni came back and sat on the couch ready to hear what I had to say. I picked my glass up and took a sip of my Ciroc Apple while getting my thoughts together. She picked up the blunt lighting it taking a couple pulls before passing it to me. When I smoked, it always relaxed me. So, after passing it back to her I began my story.

When Keith left me I sunk into depression because I couldn't believe he would do me like that. He was the love of my life so I thought. I had that day all planned out. We were going to have a romantic dinner and I was going to be dessert. When I came home from work that day I didn't know my life wouldn't be the same. I had come home and started preparing dinner I was making steak, bake potatoes, string beans and a toss salad. I seasoned and prepared my steak for the oven along with the bake potatoes. I figured while they were in the oven I could have myself a glass of wine and take a shower before I finish dinner.

Once my shower was over, I applied lotion to my body and threw on some sexy lingerie. I went back in the kitchen and finished dinner and waited for Keith to get home. I lit the candles and waited but by the time the candles melted I was furious. I tried calling his phone but the number had been changed. That's when a light bulb went off in my head and I went to our bedroom and started checking his closet, his drawers everything was gone.

I felt like a fool I started looking around for some type of note to explain where he was at and where he had gone. I couldn't comprehend he would just up and leave me without an explanation. I loved that man with everything in me and for him to just up and leave didn't make any sense.

I went back to the kitchen and tossed the food in the garbage because I had lost my appetite. I don't know when I went to sleep but when I woke up I had a terrible headache and the sun that was shining through the windows weren't making it any better. I sat up with thoughts of last night going through my mind. I had to go to work today but I was calling out shit I owned the place anyway so they can go a day with the boss not around. I made a pot a coffee, oatmeal and a bowl of fresh fruit before looking for some Advil.

After getting myself together I prepared myself for what was ahead of me. I was going to that bastard job because he had some explaining to do. I pulled up to car wash that he owned, parked my car and got out. I walked in like I normally do and boy was I surprised when I opened the door. His secretary was sitting on his desk while getting her pussy ate. They were so into it, they never heard me open the door.

"All I saw was red and started swinging on her and him" I said laughing.

"Girl, it wasn't even him! It was his partner. I was so embarrassed but what puzzle me was why he was in Keith's office when he had his own. I apologized for swinging on them and inquired where Keith was. Tony looked at me and said that Keith sold his half of the car wash to him yesterday. Then, said he was leaving town. I just stood there and cried because that bastard had all of this planned out and I was the only one who didn't have a clue about what was going on.

As the days and weeks began to go on, I became depressed and bitter. I couldn't believe this man isolated me from my family to leave me like this. I had to get myself together and run my business because I was coming to the realization that I had been played. I was too embarrassed that I let all this happen to me and had not one clue."

Toni came over and gave me hug while I wiped my eyes.

"Tamika, you don't have to keep telling me this if you don't want to" Toni said.

"No sis, I'm okay. I just need to get this all out" I told her before pouring me another drink.

Now, at this point I hated all men because of what Keith did. I started having the mindset just like them. I was on some revenge type of stuff I was tired of being taking for granted. Now I was ready for some payback. I knew men couldn't resist me so I had no problems getting their attention. I stood 5'1, caramel complexion with dark brown eyes. I wore my hair natural since my hair was curly anyway it stopped mid shoulder with the tips dyed blonde.

CHAPTER TWO

"I met Zamir at the gym I went to. He was a personal trainer and he knew his stuff. As I was watching him train some people I was getting turned on. It's been a while since I'd been touched and I just wanted him for one night. With my new confidence, I walked over to him and introduced myself to him but he already knew who I was. While he was taking me all in, he kept licking his lips. If he only knew the thoughts that were going through my mind at the time. Hearing him calling my name bought me out of my thoughts.

I gave him my number and told him he should call me soon. I didn't expect him to call me the same night but he did. We had a nice conversation and I invited him over for a night cap. I jumped in the shower and slipped into something comfortable. I had on some grey joggers, a matching tank top and some grey and white stripe ankle socks.

I put my hair in a bushy ponytail and put on a little lip gross. I was nervous as hell so I decided to smoke me a blunt to calm my nerves because I never done anything like this before. I guess they say it's a first time for everything and tonight was about to prove that. After I finished my blunt and two shots of Ciroc I was calm and horny. As soon I went to sit down my door bell was ringing.

I said a prayer asking the lord to forgive me for the sins I was about to commit tonight. I opened the door and Zamir was standing there looking good as hell. This man was so sexy I don't know if it was the weed and drink but I was ready to fuck him right at that door.

"Can I come in or are you going to stand there licking your lips all night" he said with his voice making me wetter.

"I'm sorry, come in" I said blushing. I hoped that I could pull this off because there was no turning back now.

I moved to the side so that he could walk in. He had on some black polo sweats, white tee and wheat timbs.

"Would you like something to drink?" I asked.

"Yes, let me get a glass of Cîroc if you have some" he stated. He was my kind of guy.

I went and got two glasses and the Cîroc. We sat and talked about almost anything and everything. I was starting to feel bad but I was on a mission. The Cîroc had me feeling loose so I got up and sat on his lap.

"I wouldn't do that if I was you," he taunted with lust in his eyes.

I straddled him and started kissing on his juicy lips. I felt his dick growing in his sweatpants but I acted like I didn't.

"Tamika, you see what you are doing to me" he said, as he grinded my body on his hard member.

He lifted my tank top up and started sucking on my hard nipples. The way he was sucking on them had me so wet I knew he could feel it. I got off his lap and started taking my clothes off cause now I was drunk and ready to fuck.

He waited until I was finished undressing and laid me down on the couch. He kissed me from head to toe and when he was done I was ready for the real thing.

He looked at me and said, "I hope you taste as good as you look.

I never had my pussy ate so good in my whole life, he had me seeing stars. He was a breast with his tongue so I was hoping that his dick game was just as good if not better. After I bust the best nut I ever had, I was done. I just laid there trying to catch my breath. He pulled downed his sweatpants and he was working with a little something.

His dick was about eight inches long but it was so thick. I didn't know where he was putting that thing at.

"Don't get scared, now. I promise I will take it easy on you" he said winking at me.

I thought to myself fuck it because this was a onetime thing anyway. He put on a condom and lifted my legs so I couldn't run but I little did he know, I had no intentions on running. He put the head in and took it back out so that I could get use to his size.

"Damn ma, you wet as hell" he said as pushed in inch by inch.

Once he got it all the way in, he went crazy in my pussy. I didn't think I could cum as many times as I did. We went at all night long. We had sex in every room in my house and he left me having to soak in the hot tub because he wore me out.

We kept at like that for a couple of weeks because the sex was out of this world. He wasn't the only guy I was seeing, but he was the main one. He wanted to get serious but that wasn't what I wanted. I didn't trust men and wasn't going to start just because he made me feel good. I knew that soon I would have to cut him off before his feelings got to deep.

I went out with several men but none of them held my attention until I met Donte. Donte is what people would call a pretty boy. Everything about him, yelled 'heartbreaker' but his aura is what drew me in. He was 6'4 and looked like he should be on someone runway. I thought Zamir was fine but he didn't have anything on Donte. Donte had the prettiest smile I've ever seen this man just was plain gorgeous but his eyes told a story.

I was going to the mall to find me some shoes to go with this dress I had in my closet that I wanted to wear this weekend. I was busy looking at my phone and wasn't looking were I was going when I walked right into the back of him. I was getting ready to apologize but when he turned around I was lost for words. I didn't believe in love at first sight but I knew he was going to be my husband.

"Damn beautiful, you didn't see me" he said with an attitude.

"I'm sorry, I was looking at my phone. But, you don't have to be so mean" I said rolling my eyes.

"Next time, watch where you are going or stay off your phone. What if I was somebody else and didn't want to accept your apology?" he asked smiling.

"Well, it would have just been your lost" I said walking off. Before I could walk off, he grabbed my hand and asked for my number. I tried to play hard to get but ending up giving him my number.

Well, after that we had been kicking it every day. I told Zamir that I couldn't see him any longer but he didn't take that to well and went crazy on me. He came over my house and just flipped out on me. He grabbed my neck trying to choke the life out of me.

"If my neighbor wasn't home, I wouldn't have been here to have this conversation with you" I told Toni.

"Oh, if you think that is something well you need to have you another drink because what I'm about to tell you will leave you with your mouth open."

CHAPTER THREE

Toni got up and poured her another drink before sitting back down.

"So, me and Donte kicking it and he invites me over to his parents' house for dinner. He picked me up at 5:30pm and we arrived at his parents' house, around 6:15pm. We walk in towards the kitchen where everyone is at. He started to introduce me to his brother, and guess who it is." I paused for dramatics.

"Who was it?" Toni inquired.

"It was Keith's no good ass. He was sitting there looking stupid. Before I knew it, I ran to where he was sitting and started fucking his ass up. Now, everybody looking at me like I'm crazy but I'm mad and don't care at this point. So, Donte grabs me off him and walks me towards the door so that I can cool off. As we get to the door, it rings. Donte opens it and Zamir is standing there with a crazy look in his eyes."

"Wait, are you serious?" Toni asked

"Yes, I didn't know how much more of this I could take" I told her.

"So, the next thing you know Zamir pulls out a gun and starts waving it around like a crazed lunatic. At this point, I am scared shitless. Donte is trying to talk some sense into him while I'm praying the whole time. Just as I thought Donte was getting through to him, he fires the gun and everything went black. When I came to, I was in the hospital. But, I hadn't been shot by the crazy fool. I got overexcited, passed out and hit my head.

When Zamir fired the gun, it got jammed and he took off running before the cops got there from what was told to me. The doctors kept me in the hospital that night for observation but Keith thought it was a good idea to come to the hospital with Donte. The nurse made him leave shortly afterwards because the monitors started going off from my blood pressure rising at the sight of him. I was shocked that he had the nerve to show his face after all of this time. Now, I have to explain to Donte why I went crazy on Keith's ass.

So after Keith leaves, Donte asked me what's up. I begin to tell him about me and Keith's relationship and from the look on his face he was surprised to say the least. He said he had to have a talk with his brother but what blew me away was when he revealed that Keith is married and has been married for the last four years."

"Toni, are you okay? I asked her.

"Yes. It's what you just said, it made me choke on my drink" she replied.

"I was just as surprised as you are, shit if he was still in the room I think security would have been taking him out or he would have been in the hospital."

"Girl, let me get back to the story before I lose my train of thought" I told her laughing.

"Donte stayed with me just in case Zamir tried to come back and finish me off. We really didn't do too much talking because the medicine they gave me, had me going in and out. When the morning came, the doctor came in and checked me before giving me my discharge papers. I was so happy to be going home because I didn't get any rest with the nurses coming in and out of my room.

When I arrived home, was boy was I in for a big surprise. Donte and I get to the house and everything looks normal but when we get closer we see that the door is opened. We walk in the house and my house was destroyed. All I could do was stand there and cry before thinking to check upstairs. I run upstairs to check the other rooms and my bedroom. I opened my bedroom door and I couldn't stop myself from crying.

My stuff was everywhere but what got me was the message that was on the wall. It said "I'm coming to finish what I started with you bitch, you're not just going to throw me away just like that." Now, I'm petrified because I don't know who did this. I done swung on Keith yesterday and Zamir tried to kill me. I go in my bathroom, found a dead rat in the sink, with a message taped to that read "you're next."

To be Continued.............

You can contact me @ Rasheemahw@hotmail.com
Facebook: Author Rasheemah
Twitter @realdivasoflit
IG: Lady_s89

BLESSED BY GOD
By Honey Bee

Kathy was a fourteen-year old, Caucasian girl that lived at home with both of her parents and an older sister. Her parents, heavily involved in their faith; made sure that the family went to church every Sunday and to bible study every Wednesday. Kathy, a straight 'A' student wasn't a troublesome teen and because of this; her parents trusted her to make most of her own decisions. She had a boyfriend, named Micha that she'd been dating for six months. Micha, also fourteen was African-American. He too, lived at home with both of his parents and his younger brother.

It wasn't long before Kathy begin to feel as if she would be with him forever, and after he declared his love to her; she made a life changing decision. Against what her parents and the church had instilled in Kathy, she and Micha began to have sexual relations.

Three months into their newfound intimacy, Kathy began to notice a pattern of morning illness followed by a low tolerance to her once favorite foods. Not sure what it was that could be wrong with her and too afraid to confide in her sister; Kathy told a few friends at school. Their answers were unanimous, with the suggestion that Kathy go the local clinic during one of their walk-in days and request a pregnancy test to be done. In denial about the possibility of being pregnant, Kathy prolonged her trip to the clinic. After three weeks and a missed menstrual, Kathy could no longer ignore what was looking to be the obvious.

After doing some research, Kathy found out that the clinic offered walk-in pregnancy tests on Tuesdays and Thursdays. Knowing she couldn't wait any longer, Kathy decided she would go that upcoming Thursday. Dressed in baggy sweats, a large shirt and an old fitted cap; Kathy kept a low profile as she filled out the small registration form. The clinic nurse called Kathy into a private room, passed her a small cup and a gown. She instructed Kathy to remove her undergarments, place the gown on with the opening facing the back and to give a small urine sample in the cup.

As the nurse left the room with the collected sample, Kathy sat on the table, clinching her cross necklace and saying a silent prayer. The nurse returned shortly after with the doctor. Kathy could tell by the empathetic looks on their faces, that the news she was about to receive, was just the opposite of what she'd prayed for. Regretfully, the doctor confirmed Kathy's pregnancy and after a quick ultrasound; estimated her to be about eight weeks pregnant.

Devastated, Kathy knew that she would have to hide the pregnancy from her parents. Once they found out, she knew that they would opt for her to terminate the pregnancy; in order to save face. However, Kathy did not believe in abortions and wanted to keep her baby. She'd hope that after the baby was born, her parents would fall in love with the baby and everything would work itself out.

Later that afternoon….

Micha was sitting on the sofa, watching T.V. with his brother when he received a text from Kathy.

"Babe, I just came from the clinic. The reason I've been so sick lately, is because I am pregnant. Eight weeks, to be exact. Please, call me when you get the chance.

Micha dropped his phone and yelled out, "Oh, no!"

"What's wrong with you, Micha?" his brother questioned, while staring at him awkwardly.

"Uh, nothing. It's nothing. Finish watching TV, I'll be back." Micha grabbed his phone off of the floor and ran up to his room to call Kathy.

She answered on the second ring and he could tell by the sounds of her sniffles, that she'd been crying.

"Don't cry, Kathy." He pleaded.

" I am scared, Micha. What are we going to do? We are only fourteen, we don't have jobs and we live at home with our parents. I haven't told my parents yet and I know if I do, they'll make me get an abortion. I don't want to get an abortion, Micha" Kathy sobbed.

" I wouldn't want you to, Kathy. Please stop crying, we'll figure this out. I am here with you, you are not alone. We will get through this together. Now, all I have to do is tell my parents." Micha sighed.

"Oh, no. Please don't. If you tell your parents, then they'll want to speak with my parents." Kathy reasoned.

"Let's just keep this between us until after the baby is born, then they won't have a choice but to love and accept our child."

"Are you sure, Kathy? What if that doesn't work?" Micha was concerned that her plan to hide the pregnancy wouldn't work and they'd be in bigger trouble than they already were.

"I am positive, Micha. It's the only option we have, if

we want to keep our baby. 'We' do want to keep our baby? Right?" Kathy needed Micha's reassurance.

"Yes, we want to keep our baby Kathy. I told you, I am here with you and I am not going anywhere."

"Thank you, Micha. Thank you for standing by me, I love you"

"I love you too, Kathy. Are you okay now?"

"Yes, I am fine. I am about to walk into the house, I'll call you later." Kathy hung up the phone and breathed a sigh of relief. She was happy to know that she and Micha were on the same page, and that she wouldn't go through the pregnancy alone.

****

As the months passed and the seasons changed, Kathy managed to keep her pregnancy under wraps. Mid-way into her second trimester, the morning sickness ceased and it made it a little easier on her. Being petite, Kathy carried small and mostly in her back so her baby bump was barely noticeable especially when she wore larger clothes.

It was a cold winter night when Kathy started to go into labor. Looking at her alarm clock, it was three in the morning. Unable to bare the pain, Kathy knew she had to get to the hospital; sooner rather than later. She slid her phone off the dresser, while breathing through the frequent contractions and called Micha.

"Hello," Micha sleepily whispered into the receiver.

"Micha, it's time. I need to go to the hospital"

"Are you sure?"

"Yes, I am sure!" Kathy screamed as another contraction tore through her lower body.

"Okay, okay. I am getting ready now. How are you getting there?"

"I will have to wake my sister up and she will take me. Do you want her to pick you up?"

"No, I am going to wake my parents up and tell them. They are going to kill me." Micha huffed.

"Everything will be alright, babe. I'll see you soon."

"See you soon," They hung up and prepared for the journey ahead.

Kathy crept into her sister Lena's room and tapped her awake.

"Lena, wake up. I need you to take me to the hospital" Kathy whispered.

Groggily, Lena slowly began to wake. "Take you to the hospital for what? What's wrong with you that you need to go to the hospital," Lena looked at her phone. "In the middle of the night?"

"I am in labor"

"Labor? Like in, I am having a baby kind of labor?" Lena questioned as she popped out of bed.

"Yes," Kathy answered shamefully.

"Oh, Kathy. How did you let this happen? How long have you known that you were pregnant? Why didn't you tell anyone that you were pregnant?" Lena fired off a dozen questions.

"I'll explain everything in the car. But, I really need to get the hospital now, the baby is coming!" Kathy muffled a scream as another strong contraction started.

"Okay, let me go wake up mom and dad" Lena started to walk towards her bedroom door.

Kathy jumped on her feet, "No, you can't! Just get me to the hospital and call them after the baby has been born. Please," Kathy begged.

Reluctantly, Lena agreed. Fifteen minutes later, Lena helped Kathy into the car and started heading to the hospital.

"Kathy, have you had any prenatal check- ups or anything? How are you going to support this baby? You just turned fifteen and can't get a job til' you are sixteen."

"I've been going to the clinic for my prenatal. The baby

is healthy and full term." Kathy explained. "After I have the baby, I will apply for public assistance"

Lena shook her head as she pulled into the hospital's emergency room parking lot. She ran inside and told a nurse that her fifteen-year old sister was in the car, in labor. The nurse got a wheel chair and followed her to the car. As they were helping into Kathy the wheelchair, a silver Nissan pulled up and Micha got out.

"I'm here, Kathy. Hi, Lena"

"Hi. Micha" Lena responded as she shook her head.

When Kathy looked up to greet Micha, she noticed that his mother Jackie was standing behind him.

"Kathy, where is your parents? And, why are we just now finding out that we are going to be grandparents?"

Kathy hung her head low and was about to answer when the nurse spoke up.

"I don't know what is going on but I need to get her up to labor and delivery so that the doctors can check her out. Y'all can figure everything else out after we get her situated."

"Kathy, I'll be right up as soon as I park the car" Lena said as she got back into the car.

Micha's dad, Mike had already pulled off to go find a parking spot for his car. Micha and his mother, followed behind the nurse. Once they got Kathy upstairs to the maternity section, they signed her in.

"Alright, everyone stay here in the waiting room. I'll be back with an update, shortly." The nurse instructed. As the nurse was wheeling Kathy to the back, she asked her if she'd like to call her parents.

"My sister Lena will make the call, when the time is right. Can I ask you a question?"

"Sure, Hun." The nurse replied.

"Could my parents or Micha's parents, make us give up the baby for adoption?"

"No, they can't. But may I ask, how will you manage

being a mother? You're so young."

"The best way I can, I don't have a choice; this is my baby and I will raise him or her to the best of my abilities." The nurse smiled at her and helped her into the stretcher.

"Lift up. Okay, these straps I am placing around your belly, are monitors that allow me to watch the baby's heart rate as well as the length and frequency of your contractions. I will update your family once the resident finishes with your exam. In the meantime, I am going to call your doctor and let him know that you are here." The nurse set off to do all that she needed to do.

****

It had been three hours since Kathy had been admitted into the hospital, in active labor. Micha was pacing the floor, back and forth when the nurse appeared from the back.

"She is progressing very nicely. She is now six centimeters dilated and the doctor is stripping her membranes. It shouldn't be much longer. If there are any important phone calls that need to be made, now would be the perfect time" The nurse winked in Lena's direction.

Getting the hint from the nurse, Lena decided she would call their parents and let them know what was going on. Kathy would need all of the support that she could get especially since she was entering the final stages of labor. She started speaking into the phone as soon as she heard their father's voice on the other end. Lena gave him a quick breakdown of the night's events; he was furious! Before hanging up, he asked Lena to tell Kathy that her nor her child were welcomed in their home.

As the line went dead, Lena sat with a blank stare on her face. Looking at the expression on Lena's face, Jackie could see that things were going to be bad for Kathy and the baby.

"Are they on their way? Jackie questioned as she took a seat next to Lena.

"No, they aren't. My father said that Kathy and the baby couldn't live with us. I know Kathy did wrong, but how can parents especially those who claim to serve and dedicate their lives to lord; just turn their back on their child and grandchild like that? They make us go to church every Sunday and yet in this moment, they aren't acting like Christians at all. No matter how this child was conceived, it is still a blessing from God and they refuse to see it as that." Lena cried.

Micha's mom leaned over and gave Lena a hug. Jackie attempted to call Kathy's parents herself to see is she could be a voice of reason but that was to no avail; she got the same response as Lena had gotten.

Walking back over to her son, she had no words; she could only shake her head.

"I am sorry mom. We only had unprotected sex twice, I swear. I didn't think this would happen. What will happen to Kathy and the baby?"

"Son, I don't believe in taking a child from its mother and my grandchild will not be homeless or in foster care so she will have to move in with us. She and the baby can have the guest room and the both of you have to finish school. When you each turn sixteen, you will get jobs to support your family and she will need to go on birth control so this does not happen again." Jackie spoke as she looked to her husband for confirmation.

Micha looked on at his parents with tear filled eyes, "Thank You."

Lena overheard Jackie's offer and couldn't hold back her own tears of gratitude.

"Thank you so much, for being willing to open your home to both my sister and my niece or nephew. I have a part time job and will help out with getting the baby and Kathy some things."

It was Lena's turn to lean in and give Jackie a hug. When Micha spotted their nurse coming down the hall, he jumped to his feet immediately.

"Alright, she has made it to eight centimeters and will be ready to deliver very soon. You all can come in for a short visit but only one can stay in the room with her during delivery." The group gathered their belongings and hastily followed behind the nurse to Kathy's room.

Lena walked up to her sister and gave her a comforting hug, "I'll always be here for you, Kathy. I love you"

Kathy looked into her sister's eyes and knew all was not well. "They're not coming, are they?"

Sadly, Lena shook her head as she sat on the edge of the bed. Kathy's tears ran freely from her eyes.

"Don't cry, Kathy." Lena pleaded. "Everything will work itself out. In fact, it has already worked itself out," Lena smiled at Jackie.

"What do you mean by that? How has it worked itself out? I am fifteen, and I am about to become a mother and homeless" Kathy sobbed.

"Yes, you are fifteen and you are about to become a mother but what you won't be is homeless," Jackie spoke up. "You know we wouldn't allow that. You and the baby are welcomed in our home, you will occupy the guest room. Lena is also welcomed to visit as often as she'd like. Now, there will be some ground rules but we'll discuss them later on. Right now, let's focus on getting this baby here safe and sound."

Kathy's tears quickly turned to tears of joy. She was getting ready to respond but was interrupted by a knock at the door; her obstetrician walked in.

"Kathy, it is time for me to check you again. I need everyone out except the one that is staying for the delivery."

Micha looked back and forth at his parents. He was terrified.

"Micha, now is not the time to be afraid son. You are moments from becoming a father, Kathy will need all of your support and attention during this next phase. It is time to man up, son" Micha's father spoke as he turned to leave the room. Micha nodded his head in agreement as he took a deep breath and took his position by Kathy's bedside.

An hour later, Micha reentered the waiting area.

"It's a boy." Micha announced.

"Congratulations, son" Micha's father was the first to speak.

"What is his name?" Lena asked.

"We haven't named him yet, we thought it would be nice if we all came up with a name together" Micha beamed with pride.

Everyone smiled at one another and exchanged congratulatory hugs. Micha was turning to go back into the delivery room when the nurse bust through the doors.

"There has been some complications. Lena, does Kathy have any heart conditions?"

"Uh," Lena stammered as she tried hard to think. "Yes! Yes, she was born with a heart murmur. But, the doctors said she'd be fine in life."

"Okay, her heart rate dropped dramatically after delivery. The doctors are working hard to stabilize her. I need a contact number for your parents so that we may get authorizations for any blood transfusions, surgeries, etc that may be needed." The nurse explained.

Lena, felt faint. She quickly grabbed a seat.

"This is only for precautionary measures, no need to be alarmed." The nurse added. "I'll keep you guys posted."

Half an hour later, the nurse returned.

"Kathy is stable and the baby is healthy. However, the delivery put a lot of strain on Kathy's heart. She will need to see a cardiologist before she can be cleared. I've already paged him and he'll be up shortly."

"Were you able to get in contact with my parents?" Lena

inquired.

"Unfortunately, I did." The nurse replied.

"What did they say? Are they on their way?"

"Your father wasn't the most pleasant man to speak with. Upon informing him of Kathy's complications, his response was; Kathy is an adult now and would have to deal with her own issues. He also asked me to tell you, Lena that if you'd like to continue living under their roof; you should return home immediately." The nurse shook her head in disbelief.

"Unbelievable! I can't believe they are turning their back on her like this. I don't know if I want to live under the same roof as them, they disgust me." Lena shook her head. "May I see my sister and nephew before I leave?"

"Sure, it will have to be quick because she's still in recovery."

Three days later, Kathy and her newborn baby Kyle were released from the hospital. As Kathy got out of the car and carried Kyle into their new home; she got the shock of her life.

"Surprise!" a crowd greeted her as she entered the livingroom.

Her sister, with the help of Micha and his parents; gathered as many friends and family members as they could and put together a "Welcome Home" baby shower.

"Wow! Thank you so much everyone" Kathy smiled with tears in her eyes. She was overwhelmed with joy and felt truly blessed for the people that she had in her life. She was still heartbroken about her parents, but she knew she did what was best for her; and that was Kyle.

****

As time went by, Kathy and Micha did just as they'd promised. They went to school, got part time jobs and raised Kyle to the best of their abilities. Micha's parents and Lena, helped out as much as they could with babysitting and buying whatever else Kyle needed. A year and a half later, both Micha and Kathy finished high school with honors. As a graduation gift, Micha's parents paid the deposit on an apartment, east of Richmond for the young family.

Kathy and Micha were thrilled about having their own apartment. They moved in to their new home, shortly after Kyle's second birthday. Things were beginning to look up for the young couple, Micha got hired at the hospital as a Janitor; making sixteen dollars an hour. The position came complete with health insurance for the entire family, paid vacations and holiday pay. Kathy, secured the fulltime sectary positon at the office she'd been tempting at.

Their schedules worked perfectly. Micha worked the night shift, 11pm to 7am and Kathy worked the day, 9am to 4pm. They never had to worry about a childcare bill. After a few months, they were able to save enough money to buy a car. Which helped by cutting the travel time to and from their jobs in half, giving them a little more time to spend with each other as a family.

****

One blazing summer night, Micha kissed Kathy and Kyle goodnight as he headed out to work. Kathy sat Kyle on the living room floor as she began to cleanup.

As she was picking up Kyle's play castle, gunshots rang out. Quickly, she dodged for cover, with Kyle tucked securely under her. Although hearing gunshots in their neighborhood wasn't uncommon, Kathy got an eerie feeling. Slowly, she raised her head to look out their front window. She saw a man running away and two men sprawled out in the street. When she saw Micha's work bag laying on the curb, she screamed and went into panic mode.

She grabbed Kyle and ran out the door. She dashed

down the stairs and out of the complex.

"Mommy, what wrong?" Kyle wailed.

There was no time to answer him, she needed to get to where she saw Micha's bag. When she reached his bag, he was nowhere in sight. Scared, she walked around the car to where she'd seen the two men laying in the street. When she saw the "Janitor" label, she lost it.

She put Kyle down and ran over to where Micha was lying on the ground. She turned him over and there was blood seeping from his stomach.

"Oh my God! Micha don't die, please don't die!"

She reached in her pocket and dialed 911.

"Hello, 911 operator. What is your emergency?"

"My boyfriend has been shot! They shot him!" Kathy screamed into the phone hysterically.

"Okay, ma'am. You have to calm down. Can you tell me where he is shot at?"

"I think in his stomach, please help him!"

"What is your location? I am dispatching an ambulance to you, right now."

Kathy gave the operator the address of their complex. The ET advised Kathy to keep Micha alert for as long as she could.

"Micha! Micha, can you hear me baby?" Kathy shook Micha's still body. "Micha, I need you to say something. Baby, please!" Kathy begged.

"Daddy, wake up! Mommy's crying." Kyle tapped his father's face.

Micha reached his hand out and touched Kyles face, "I love you, son." Then he looked at Kathy. "I love you too, baby. Take care of our son." Was the last thing he said before he closed his eyes. Kathy went ballistic.

"No! Micha you can't close your eyes. Wake up, we need you!" Just then, she heard the sirens of the ambulance.

The technicians jumped out of the truck and rushed over to Micha. One of the technician's ripped opened Micha's shirt, located his wound and started to apply gauzes. While the other, searched for a pulse.

"I found one, it's weak though." She shouted.

"We need to get him to the hospital, immediately! He's lost a lot of blood" the other responded. They picked Micha up and placed him on a gurney with an oxygen mask on his face.

"Ma'am will you be riding with him?" The technician asked as he climbed aboard the truck.

"No, I'll follow behind you" Kathy responded.

She grabbed the car keys that were left behind from where Micha had been laying. She put Kyle in his car seat and followed the ambulance to the hospital.

While on the way, she called Micha's parents and told them what had happened.

"Oh my god! Is he okay?" Jackie screamed into the phone.

"He lost a lot of blood but they found a weak pulse on the scene. We are heading to the hospital, right now."

"Oh my god! Thank you for calling us, Kathy. We're on our way." Jackie hung up the phone.

Once she ended the call, she dialed her boss's number. She briefly explained the situation and asked for the day off. Her boss agreed, and wished her the best of luck.

Kathy parked the car, quickly grabbed Kyle and ran over to the ambulance as they pulled Micha from the back.

The technicians raced through the Emergency Room doors with Kathy following closely behind. A trauma code was called in over the loud speaker as Micha was rushed into the emergency operating room. Kathy looked on as the metal doors closed in front of her. She said a lengthy prayer, asking that the love of her life be returned to her and their son.

Worrisome, Kathy was sitting in the waiting room with Kyle, awaiting the arrival of Micha's parents; when two detectives walked up to Kathy.

"Good Evening, Ms. Wilson. I am Detective Reynolds and this is my partner, Detective Osborne. May we have a word with you?" Kathy gave a nod.

"My partner and I, just came from the scene. According to several witnesses, Micha was an innocent by stander who got caught in the cross fire of two other men that were arguing. One of the two men, died on the scene. The other, we are still searching for. But, don't you worry. We will catch him." Detective Reynolds assured.

Kathy thanked the officer before asking, "How is Micha? I have been sitting out here for a while and all they want to know is if he has insurance. Micha is my best friend and the father of my son. He and his family were there for me when mine turned on me and my son. If I lose him, I will die. Why won't anyone tell me anything?" Kathy tried to fight the tears but couldn't anymore.

Kyle was confused by his mother's tears.

"Mommy, where daddy? He go to get his boo-boo fixed? Huh, mommy?" Kathy couldn't say anything more, she wrapped her arms around and hugged her son tight.

"Unfortunately, I don't know. But, I will got get an update and come right back." As the Detective walked away, Jackie and Mike walked up.

"Kathy, how is our son?" Jackie asked, as the tears threatened to escape from her brims.

"Grandma, Grandpa! Mommy keeps crying and daddy has a big boo-boo and he was bleeding! I want to go home." Kyle said out loud.

"Oh, Kyle. Daddy is going to be okay, sweetie. Come here, baby" Jackie reached her arms out to receive her grandchild.

Mike pulled Kathy to the side so she could fill him in.

"They haven't told me anything as of yet but the Detective just went to get an update. He should be back in a few minutes.

"How did this happen, Kathy?" Mike questioned.

"The detective said that the bullet wasn't intended for Micha. He was just in the wrong place at the wrong time, and got struck by a stray bullet meant for another man." Kathy explained.

"Oh, here comes the detective now. Hopefully, he'll have some good news." Kathy spoke as she and Micha's parents walked over to the detective.

"This Micha's parents, Jackie and Mike Foster. Jackie and Mike, this is Detective Reynolds." Kathy made the introduction. "So, any updates? Is he alive? Will he be okay" Kathy rambled on with a ton of questions.

Detective Reynolds interrupted her, "Micha is still in surgery. There has been some slight damage to his intestines, that they are repairing. That's all I have for right now. Someone will be out shortly to escort you all to the ICU" He handed Kathy and Micha's parents his card with all his information on it.

"I will be in touch, soon. If you have any questions or concerns beforehand, please feel free to contact me." He turned and walked away.

A nurse came out about twenty minutes later and escorted them all to the fourth floor waiting room.

"I'll be back with an update shortly. In the meantime, please make yourselves comfortable."

Kyle was getting fussy, Kathy was an emotional wreck and Jackie paced the floor. Mike was the only one holding it together.

The nurse came back, fifteen minutes later.

"Micha's surgery was a success. The doctor will be out shortly to discuss of few things with you."

"Thank you," Mike thanked the nurse.

"Grandpa, I hungry" Kyle spoke as he tapped on Mike's leg.

Mike picked Kyle up, "As soon as grandpa finishes talking to the doctors, we'll go get you something to eat. Okay?"

Kyle nodded his head, "Can I see daddy?"

"You can see him, later on. Okay?"

"No!" Kyle got upset. "I give daddy a Band-Aid for his boo-boo"

"The doctor gave him a Band-Aid and you can see him later. He is taking a nap right now. Okay?" Mike assured him.

"Okay," Kyle smiled at his grandfather.

"Who is here with Micha Foster?" A doctor called out.

"I am Kathy Wilson, Micha's girlfriend. And, these are his parents Mr. and Mrs. Foster." Kathy answered.

The doctor asked if he was able to speak with all of them and Mike told the doctor that they were all family and to go ahead and speak.

"Although Micha's surgery was a success, as you know he lost a lot of blood. We may need blood from a family member. Is there anyone that is willing to donate if it comes to that?"

Mike told the doctor that he would.

"Great, now on to a more serious issue. When the bullet hit Micha, it entered his stomach, did some damage to his intestines and got stuck in his kidney. We've repaired the intestines and have removed the bullet from the kidney, however that kidney may not function again. We will have to keep him for at least a week, to keep an eye on him. If the kidney fails, he will need dialysis unless a replacement kidney is available."

"Will he survive?" Kathy inquired.

"We expect him to make a full recovery, if the kidney heals properly. If it doesn't heal, he will have a journey ahead of him but he will live. He's in recovery right now, in a hour he'll be in a regular room. At the time, you may visit him."

"What about Kyle? Will he be able to see his father?" Mike asked the doctor.

"I usually don't like young kids in the ICU rooms but

given the circumstances, for a short visit I will allow it."

"Thank you, Doctor."

As the doctor left, Mike picked up Kyle. "I am going to McDonald's. Would either of you like something?" Both ladies shook their head no.

"Alright, We'll be back soon." He and Kyle walked out of the waiting room hand in hand while Kathy and Jackie stayed, hoping to be able to see Micha.

****

Thirty minutes later, Mike and Kyle entered back into the waiting room.

"Have you been able to see Micha yet?"

"No, still nothing. I hope everything is alright," Jackie replied to her husband.

"I am certain that everything is fine. They just have to get him settled into his room.

As if she'd been watching from behind a hidden door, a nurse appeared.

"Family of Micha Foster, you may begin your visit.

"Kathy, you and Kyle go in first. We'll be right here" Jackie insisted.

Kathy mouthed the words 'Thank You' as she took Kyle by the hand and followed the nurse.

The nurse slowly opened the door, "He's still under the effects of the medications. So, he'll be in and out of it."

"Okay," Kathy answered as she walked in. First thing she noticed was all of the tubes and monitors attached to Micha.

"Mommy, why the wires on daddy?" Kyle inquired.

"They are there, so the doctors can watch how daddy is doing when they are not in here."

Micha must have heard Kyle because he opened his eyes. He patted the bed, insisting that Kathy bring Kyle to sit alongside of him. Kathy wanted to protest against the idea, afraid Kyle might detach an important wire but she couldn't say no to Micha. She picked Kyle up and placed him on the edge of the bed.

"Daddy, how did you get that boo-boo?"

"I am fine, Kyle. Daddy just has to be quicker on his feet like you," he teased Kyle as he tickled his belly.

"Kathy, I am sorry you had to miss a day out of work. Make sure you go for rest of the week. I am going to be out for a while and we have to pay the bills. I'll ask my mom to watch him till I get out of here."

"Are you sure? I can figure something else out."

"Yes, go to work tomorrow."

"Alright, but Lena will help with babysitting so your mom doesn't have to do it all the time. I will call her later."

"Daddy, Aunt Lena lets me eat tacos with extra cheese."

Micha nodded his head at Kyle and looked up at Kathy and apologized again about her being out of work.

"I am not worried about work. I was so scared that I'd lost you Micha. Don't ever scare me like that again! I don't know what I would do without you. You and Kyle are my life." Kathy tried to hold the tears back but couldn't.

Micha reached for her hand. "I am sorry Kathy. I never meant to scare you. What did the doctor say about my recovery time?"

"He told us that you lost a lot of blood and he didn't know if your kidney was going to be ok. He wants to keep you here for a week, to monitor your healing process. Your mom and dad are out in the waiting room, waiting their turn to see you. I am just so grateful that God answered my prayers and protected you."

Micha smiled at her, "I love you, Kathy." She could tell that he was getting sleepy.

Bending down, she kissed his lips lightly, "I love you too, Micha. Kyle and I are getting ready to leave out so that your parents can come in, okay?" Micha nodded his head.

"I give daddy a kiss too?" Kyle asked.

"Of course you can, baby. Be careful, though."

With the help of Kathy, Kyle leaned over and gave Micha a kiss and hug.

"Okay, now get up daddy. It's time for you to come home with me." Kyle spoke as he tapped his father's face.

Kathy picked him up, "Daddy has to stay the night, Kyle." Kyle started to cry. Kathy did her best calming him down, even though she wanted to cry herself.

****

A week later, Micha was on the sofa with Kyle watching T.V. while Kathy was cooking dinner; there was a sudden rang of the doorbell. Micha got up from the sofa, ringed the buzzard and waited by the door. Peeking through the peephole, Micha recognized Detective Reynolds from the hospital.

"Good evening, Detective. How can I help you?"

"Hey there, Micha. It's good to see you on your feet. I just wanted to stop by and tell you that we have apprehended the man who shot you. He admitted to firing the gun in self-defense. When I told him that not only killed the other guy but that he'd hit an innocent by-stander, he broke down. He said, he never meant to hurt anyone. He was only trying to stop the man from robbing him. He is currently under arrest for Murder, attempted murder, reckless endangerment, and illegal use of a firearm."

"Wow! Thank you for the update, Detective Reynolds."

"No problem, Micha. Be expecting a visit from a deputy, soon. He'll be giving you a summons to attend to court." The two men, shook hands and said their goodbyes.

"Who was that at the door, hun?" Kathy asked, as Micha reentered the living room.

"That was Detective Reynolds. He stopped by to let us know that they caught the guy who shot me." Kathy was glad to hear that but could tell that it bothered Micha.

"What's wrong, Micha?" Kathy pried.

"I just hate the fact that I am being summoned to court to testify. I do not want to be part of the reason that another black man goes to prison.

"But Micha, you are not the reason. You are the victim. You didn't not place the gun in that man's hand. You didn't put his finger on the trigger and make him shoot that man. And, you didn't ask to be shot."

"I know all of that Kathy. But, you just won't ever understand" Micha spoke as he reclaimed his spot on the sofa.

Kathy shrugged her shoulders. She couldn't understand why Micha wouldn't help the detectives but she was happy that she had little family back together. Smiling, she went back into the kitchen. She was finishing up her specially planned dinner, for the two men God had blessed her with; Micha and their beautiful son Kyle.

AVAILABLE TITLES BY HONEY BEE

Love on The other side
Love on the same side
He Saved Me
Carolina Shot Caller

COMING SOON

The urban chronicles (an urban magazine)
Beneath the river

FIRSTBORN DESIGNS

WHEN POPS DIED
By RR Moore

When Pops died, I didn't cry/ I didn't know him that well/ he sent me some money on Christmas and birthdays, but I hadn't seen him since I was 12/ Now I'm 19, and not likely to front/Pops died driving drunk/crashed his brand new truck/ meanwhile, I got two bullshit jobs/ and my life is fucked/Wendy's and Burger King, one pair of work jeans/hurting/and to keep it real, I'm not sad/ At the same time, my older brother was raised by dad/ but what makes me mad/is that when I turned 16, I got a card with $500 inside/while he got a car and a party and I wasn't invited/ I'm the secret child we separated by 300 miles/

But we both David's child, he's Devin and I'm Miles/ I never been wild, but from how I know him, Devin he a loose cannon/Only two years older than me you should see the money he handling/I'm not just talking his posts on Instagram and Facebook/He is the MAN, meanwhile I'm trying to teach Tank to cook/Tank is my little brother, 11 and he fuss a lot/ Mom doing a double at the restaurant/she waitress and receive tips... I get Tank sent off to school and do dishes.

DEVIN
Shit so crazy, I'm devastated, distraught and depressed/

Pops gone now shit is a mess/hard to keep going but I'm
doing my best/It's been just me and Pops since my mom's
death/a couple years ago cancer took her last breath/once
she died Pops got to hustling extra hard/I got to hustling
extra hard as well and we bought matching cars/just me and
him we ain't need no squad, all cash no Visa card/ Now
he's gone and I realize my reach ain't that long/ Cause
niggaz ain't returning my calls since the street heard David
gone/ No shoulder to lean on/to cry, I drink and drive/ don't
know what to think inside/ I'm 21 and alone, dry ass phone,
fly ass home/but without Pops I don't even want to go on/
Tomorrow is the funeral but then what's next.

I don't even know where Pops keeps the drugs and
never met the connect/and his phone was destroyed in the
accident/went to Pops' crib and someone had broken in and
crashed the shit/ I had keys to all of his whips/I searched all
three and ain't find shit.

I got a lot of bitches cause of my cash flow/but no
homies cause I'm an arrogant asshole/Which is accepted
when your Pops is the plug/But not he's gone and the
streets aren't showing any love/I know exactly what my
worth is, and I carry it all in my pockets/34k and 4 ounces,
I roll down my window and pour Remy out it.

MILES

Funeral flow/ Momma finally convinced me I should go/
I put on my only suit and took three buses, now I'm here
for the show/ Coming through the parking lot I felt the
weight of my world on my shoulders/ Parking lot full of
foreign cars plus a red Range Rover/that's Devin's truck/I
recognize it from Instagram, plus his name is on it...I walk
in and everyone turns when the door shuts.

DEVIN

I turn around and there goes Miles, looking like a little
me/ with a too small suit and beat up Nikes/I ain't even call

him about Pops funeral and I guess that was wrong of me/He has grown since the last time I seen him and now he is taller than me/he walked down the aisle and we hugged, it was fake to me/Pops death dug a hole in my heart, and there is no vacancy/walked over he looks over to the casket/ I moved out his way, I had my time I'll let him have it...

MILES

It felt like fake love, smelled like weed and cologne/church was practically packed yet I feel all alone/ Walked to Pops casket on my own/poker face, no emotion shown/Pops beard had grown and he had more meat on his bones/in the past 7 years we both had physically grown/I took my time, I wanted to remember his face/he was fresh as hell, in his open casket Pops always had good taste/meanwhile I poke holes in my belt to keep my pants on my waist/It wasn't hate it was honesty/I didn't think it would bother me/cause even though today was his funeral he's been dead to me/

Devin stands next to me/and his tears pour/I wanna be there for him/even though I barely know him/I overhear someone say Devin you will be ok?/and selfishly I feel like I am in the way,/besides Devin I don't know anyone here anyway/ I no longer want to stay they praying and crying/I see some realizing who I am/Temperatures rising/I slide in a pew and put on my sunglasses/seems like forever but only an hour passes/

Devin is like "let's go to the cemetery/I will pass, he acting like his feelings hurt, as we approach his truck/I explain I don't want to hurt his feelings but he should respect mine as such/Plus, my bus arrives in a few minutes/Told him I will inbox him and that he can go handle his business/This is where we should depart with a hug and some dap...but he just shrugs, pulls out his keys and showed me his back.

A few weeks passed/I called Devin a couple times but no reply back/that's fine with me no reason to change up now/same shit round my way but it's worse now/fired from Burger King so it's one job now/ and we hurting/ Moms still working but her boss is an aggressive asshole/things you have to do for the cash flow.

I'd been out looking for jobs now I'm back home helping Tank with his homework/Mom comes in from work and checks the mailbox, and there's a letter from a lawyer/I almost never get mail so this was not expected/you can't know how surprised I was when I read it/apparently Pops left me a car that the lawyer got/if that's true he probably left Devin a car lot/hard to believe/and Moms told me to call and see, once my address was confirmed basically the car belonged to me/

All I had to do was sign when it arrived/he assured me it was in good shape, a Malibu 2005/that'll be super smooth if this ain't no jive/ Tank works back and forth to school and its getting cold outside/the irony/a deadbeat all my life but in the after-life he provides for me/and as bad as we need a whip/I ain't even gone trip/but 'I'll believe it when I see it/

Shit I'm used to disappointment so imagine my excitement when Monday came/ tow truck brought the Chevy and I received the keys once I signed my name/calm down Miles I told myself as my adrenaline raced/ put the key in the ignition and said a prayer just in case/ she started with no problem, officially my first car/ First thing I did was drove to Mom, lunch time was always busy at the restaurant/ I found a spot to wait until she could pull herself away/

I watched her slave/ customers mispronouncing her name/ then I started watching her tips it was petty change/ it's cool cuz now we got us a whip but we need better days/ Mama got greys in her hair/ shoes scuffed up she need a new pair/ we both got hand me downs but we make sure

Tank got new gear/ he's been fresh all school year/ finally she catches a break and can sit still for a minute/

I tell her about the car all black with rims and the windows tinted/ she brought me back to Earth asking how we gone keep gas in it/ that's just like Mom always giving out lessons/ she said if you got it off of sin it's not a blessing/ but I ain't stressing/ this car gone get me to a second job/I asked if she wanted me to pick her up from work tonight/ but she said she would ride with Mr. Clark and be alright/ have a good night I told her as I kissed her forehead/ she smiled and hoped she'd be home before Tank went to bed/

On my way out I bumped into Mr Clark, Wassup old head?/ Only way to not end up old is to end up dead./ We laughed and Mr. Clark gave me a shoulder bump/ him and Mama try to front like they just friends but we know what's up/ he showed me some things/ plus took Tank to wrestling matches and to skating rinks/ him and mom been dealing with each other since I was 17/ Mr. Clark had one son, Jason/and Jason was into everything, while Mr. Clark was cooking at the restaurant/

Jason cooked up for the block and had the game on lock/ the only friend I got/ he took me with him to the gambling spot/ whenever he would win he'd gimme half off top/ whenever we linked up he'd ask if Tank was straight/ he held me down like a paperweight/I couldn't wait to show him how the tables had turned/ pulled up to his trap house where his paper got earned/ so we dipped and rode, that's my guy so I let him drive/he had a box Chevy on 26's but had to admit this was fly/

His phone steady buzz/ he gotta make a few runs/ wouldn't be the first time I was shotgun/ Now Jason wasn't rich, wasn't running through bricks/ he had a few thousand maybe but he ain't never had six/ ridiculous/ the difference between Wendy's and pack pushing is just a couple of inches/ So we bent a few corners/ gas was low Jason gave me thirty dollars/ a few more runs and it was time to holla/ straight to do crib to meet Tank when he came home/ and I couldn't resist taking pics of the whip on my phone/Posted a few pics on my *Facebook* page, once I put them up/I realized I had never popped the trunk…

DEVIN

I woke up to watch Sports Center and the cable turned off/ on top of that the connect won't call back/ it's all whack/ I done damn near fell off and trying to crawl back/ Done broke these ounces to all packs/ to combine to my small stack/ It's niggas out here that know they owe Pops/everyone I call gives me a story about what they don't got/Tough talk won't work/ I'm reduced to hoping they do the right thing/ less than likely/ Pops was a loose cannon but that ain't like me/ I'm smooth sailing and avoid confrontations/ and Pops had it so good I never bothered to save what I was making/

And just this fast its taking a toll, the reign is over/ just thankful I don't owe no money on the Range Rover/ can't stand being sober/ and I don't know how to go forward/ try to talk to Pops lawyer but he wants a retainer/ I done got too far in the water/ and no lifeguard to save me/ low on paper and getting low on self- esteem, time to come up with a scheme/ once I come up with a sucker to sell a dream/ I hit the block and got robbed by a fiend/ this the worst dream/More like a nightmare/Pops gone I'm all alone and it's not fair/ try to find love in the streets but it's not there/

Back home I sit on the stairs and contemplate /Miles been calling and texting but that can all wait/ miss me with that brother shit It's too late/ he too fake, annoying like mosquitos bites and tooth aches/so I sent him to voicemail, he can go to hell/ 'I'm a mutha fuckin monster and he don't know me… Oh the fuck well…..

MILES

Man I opened up that trunk and couldn't believe my eyes/so I shut it back and sighed/wiped my eyes and gave it another try/ same results I feel my heart pulse racing/ I start pacing, damn near hyper ventilating/ I ain't know what to do so I hit up Jason/ told him I had a problem and could he come through/ he said he had some runs and to give him an hour or two/ Tank came home I made him take a shower and fix his food/ then I set him up doing homework in the living room/ an hour passed I'm in the window watching the car out back/ low-key shook when police rode past/ and finally he comes/ Jason smoking a blunt/ on the phone with a random chic/

I led him to the car and instructed him to sit/ He had no idea what I was dealing with at all/ so I showed him, you should have seen how quick he hung up the call/ Where did you get this from? From the trunk and there is more in the duffle bag/ Nigga you got a get out of the hood starter pack, all day you rode around with that?

From there it went amazingly fast/Jason showed me everything and I took notes in Drug Class/ 2 friends with 10 bricks and no cash/ but Jason knew every trick from the pot to the bag/ and it took us all night, good thing Mom decided to stay over Mr. Clark's/ we kept running out of baggies, finally we finished with 75 ounces ready/ $1,500 a pop all profit/ and we split in dead down the middle we partners/ 10 bricks with just a little mix we kept the product proper/ And you know what they say, proper preparation prevents poor performance/ he schooled me on this dirty game with cops crooks and informants/

We both knew this wasn't meant for me but fuck it, it's here now/ I ain't seen Pops in 7 years now/ I know this was for Devin here…but I don't care/ and neither did Jason/ ain't no need to be patient/ I went back to work that night like nothing happened/ while Jason hit the block and he was about that action/ We wanted it gone in two months but Jason did it in half of that/ no reason to over price we gave out deal cause it was free to us… imagine that.

DEVIN

So I'm bored and almost broke/ done downgraded from the Range Rover to Monte Carlo/ parking lot of the pawn shop ready to pawn Pops Movado/ when I bumps into my homie Johnny Bravo/Bravo offers me $200 to ride with him/ he's headed outta town to cop some work and need somebody to ride with him/ I get it and I need the bread so I'm G for it/ an hour later we in a Wendy's parking lot and Bravo got his seat pushed forward/

I'm in the perfect position to be nosey and I'm perched and listening/Some nigga named Jason and I swear that looks like Miles with him/The transaction was quick and we was in and out/and I'll be damned if Bravo didn't say Peace to Jason and then to Miles/ Shit is wild/ and I'm figuring it out/ ended up in a rage and now I'm stalking his house/ with a hoodie a hat and shades/ I'm parked in an alley by his house a few houses away…

MILES

Jason did not lie/this the 3rd time I've seen that Monte Carlo parked outside/ now I'm peeking out the blinds as Jason was outside creeping up the strange Monte Carlo passenger side…

DEVIN

Posted in the alley waiting for opportunity/ couldn't believe the way my brother and Pops was screwing me/ You had to be blind not to see where this was going/ the reason I'm holding/ a fully loaded pistol in my lap/ this nigga just done took my life and I'm here to get it back/ From the shadows where I'm at I can see his silhouette/ been spying on him for 3 days and he ain't seen me yet/ but this the 3rd time he done looked out his blinds/ but then again I'm definitely high out my mind/ but then I heard a weapon get cocked right behind me/ heard a pop and then my shoulder disappeared beside me/ another pop and a bright white light appeared to guide me/ blood everywhere, soul and body separate and divide…then it was silence forever when the pops died.

- RR More

Facebook-Rausea Moore

AVAILABLE ON LULU.COM
Rest In Greed
Resurrected In Riches
After The Eulogy

LOCKDOWN LUST
By Kisha Green

Gateway Edna Mahan Correctional Facility

The rookie officer step through the gate, tall and stern. Grant Johnson, stands at 6'5 tall with an athletic built. His uniform shirt grips his sculpted biceps and the body of the uniform shirt is tapered with a custom fit. The crop of his jet black hair is silky, thick and wavy. The thick dark coat of hair, makes up a full beard as well. As he steps along the tier, the smell of his Burberry cologne attracts all the women inmates to the gates of their cells.

That alone, with the fact that they have his schedule down pact, from the exact days down to the exact time. This is only his third week on the job, and the female inmates can smell the fresh meat. They also can smell the milk behind his ears, which attract them even more. He's twenty-seven years old but doesn't look a day over eighteen.

As he struts confidently along the tier, the women all make way to the gates of their cells to watch and admire him. Some of them are dressed in jailhouse lingerie, hoping to catch his eye. Some are dressed in bra and panty sets while others are in boy shorts and wife beaters. All of them indulge in their best sexy impersonation.

"Officer," says the woman in the cell to the right of him. He looks over to see a beautiful young woman, dressed in only a t-shirt and no sign of a thread of panties on. Her face is made up like a runway model.

"I'm feeling sick. I may need you to take me to the doctor, I feel a bug coming down. May be a love bug," she says puckering her lips and winking her eye at him.

"May just be the flu," he replies, disregarding her attempt of seducing him. "Put some clothes on. You will be alright."

As he continues on, he keeps his eyes focused straight ahead in order not to get caught in any of their traps. He finally makes it to his desk, where he takes a seat and takes a long sigh. As soon as he seats himself in comfort, the trustee appears in front of the desk. She holds a container in her hand. She locks eyes with him, batting her long lashes.

"I saved this for you," she says as she hands over the container.

"What's that?"

"It's a piece of my birthday cake. I saved the last piece for you," she says with seduction in her eyes.

"Today is your birthday? How old are you now?"

"Twenty-one. I'm legal now," she adds.

He looks her up and down admiring her young and tender body. He views her as a piece of barely ripened fruit. Her perky nipples peek through the white t-shirt. His eyes bounce from breast to breast before landing in between the cleavage line that peeks over the v-line shirt. For a second or two his mind entertains naughty thoughts of the two of them.

His eyes travel on down to the tiny fitted gym shorts that she's wearing. The bulge in the crotch area of the shorts sits up like a clenched fist. The camel toe looks more like the mouth of Jaws, eating up the terry cloth shorts.

She feels him falling into her trap. She squeezes her legs together tightly, strangling his eyes in between her juicy thighs.

"So, you are gonna eat the cake or not?" she asks.

His eyes finally free themselves from her web. He stares into her eyes with the coldest look that he can muster under the tempting circumstances.

"I don't eat sweets," he says before looking away and looking at the newspaper that's in his hand.

Sadness fills her eyes just before they fill up with tears. "I saved it just for you." She pouts like a baby.

For a moment, he actually believes that she really means well and maybe not all of this was bait for him. Her tears actually make him feel saddened. He can see the innocence in her teary eyes. Just a young woman in a bad situation. He allows his mind to wonder what could bring such a beautiful young woman to a place like this.

He looks at the cake that she holds in her hand and then takes another look at the slice of cake in the crotch of her shorts. He would much rather dive his face in between her thighs, mouth first. He realizes that he must cut off conversation with her. The longer she stands here the more forbidden thoughts that race through his mind.

"Ok, leave it," he says. "I may snack on it later."

"I would love that," she says with a seductive grin. She places the container on the desk.

"Have a goodnight, Officer Jackson." she says as she turned around and walks away from the desk. The load, that she carries, is a wide one. Her rear end was so huge it appears impossible for such a small frame to carry it all. He watches as the tiny shorts creep up further and further, revealing more cheek with every step. Halfway across the room the shorts have disappeared into a thong, jammed in between her crack. Her entire ass now in clear view.

She looks over her shoulder and to no surprise to her at all, she has his full attention.

"If you need me, call me. I'm here at your disposal, for whatever" she says with a sly wink. Embarrassingly, he lowers his eyes onto his newspaper. When he peeks up again she has disappeared.

Now that the distraction is out of the way, he commences to doing his job and that is making sure everything is in order on the tier. He looks over to the cell across the room which is the very reason why his station is positioned here. The woman in that particular cell is reportedly the most dangerous female inmate in all of the countries. That title alone makes her detrimental to all the other inmates. Her movement is limited and she's only allowed out of her cell to shower.

He's been warned about this inmate from day one but in all of his time, here so far he can't imagine her being of any danger. To the naked eye, she appears harmless. Right now she's doing what she does all the time and that's ballet dancing. May seem quite normal except for the fact that she's naked doing it.

She refuses to wear clothes and nothing, they do, has been effective in getting her to put any on. She's known throughout the prison as Naked Lucy with Lucy short for Lucifer. Her nudity has nothing to do with entrapping male officers. She's been nude her entire prison term.

At forty-five years of age, she's been locked up for over half of her life. At twenty-one years of age, she was charged with the murder of her abusive long term boyfriend. The murder could've probably been justified and downgraded had it not been for the gruesome details. She tied him to the bed while sleeping. He awoke with her standing over him with tears in her eyes and a box cutter in her hand. After all of his begging and pleading she commenced to severing his privates off.

As if that wasn't enough, she sets him to flame and left him to die in a blaze. When police arrived she was sitting across the street from their home, waiting for them. She didn't put up a fight. As they got out of the car she assumed the position by turning around with her hands on her back. Lawyers urged her to plead insanity, but she wouldn't. She instead told judges she was in her right state of mind.

Over the years, her mental state has been verified as insane. Officials have labeled her insanely dangerous and vicious. With all of the prepping, that he's had he still can't view her as anything but harmless. All, he sees, is a woman who minds her business in the world of her own.

She does what she loves and that is ballet. She was an Alvin Ailey Dancer and model before the disaster. Her free will nudity comes from her modeling days. She never viewed her body with shame. She's always been an exhibitionist who enjoyed showing her body. At a young age, she learned that her body could take her places that she didn't believe her mind could.

Any man can understand why she could possibly believe that. Standing at five feet, ten inches tall, she has the perfect model height. Long and slender legs that seem to never end. Her beautiful legs are picture perfect. Sculpted calves, tree trunk thighs, and a beautiful apple bottom make up her lower half. A tiny waistline, flat tummy and enormous breast make up her top half.

Her dark skin, full lips, broad nose and chinky eyes make her look like a beautiful African Queen. She wears a huge natural blowout afro, kinky and course in texture. The paperwork in her file paints a picture of a vicious killer of a woman but to see her, the picture of one of the most beautiful black women in the world is painted right before your eyes.

The officer watches as she struts throughout the tiny cell on her tippy toes with grace. She stops in the middle of the cell with her arms high in the air. She poses without moving for a half a minute before she twirls around elegantly. She stops and looks up at the ceiling before dashing off on her toes. Her butt, tight and firm with barely any jiggle.

She stops at the wall, smacking both hands against it. She looks to the left then to the right before lifting her leg in the perfect six 'o clock position. She spins around on the axis of one foot. With her leg still in the air, holding it by her ankle, she stares straight ahead with poise.

She lowers her leg slowly. She slides down the wall with her arms stretched out, palms up. She looks up to the sky, making her palms meet. Her hands in a praying position she slowly lowers them to her face.

She stands up slowly, turning her head in a circle. Once she's standing firmly on both feet, she begins to belly dance with a sexual flare. The officer watches with lustful eyes admiring her beautiful body. He's hypnotized by the swaying of her thick nipples. Side to side and in circles, he follows them until he's in a slight trance. Her huge breasts lay over her washboard stomach. Her curvaceous hips explode from her tiny waistline.

Without warning, she takes off running on her toes. Her breast bounce vibrantly. She stops at the middle floor and twirls for many seconds before tippy toe walking into the cage. She grabs hold of the bars and stares ahead like an innocent caged animal in the zoo.

Tears drip down her face slowly. She lowers her body to the floor, still holding onto the bars. She flings her head back as the tears continue to pour from her eyes. She snaps her head forward and allows her hands to slide down the bars. She allows her body to collapse onto the floor.

She lays there flat on her belly, still as a statue for almost a minute. She jerks her body as she slaps the floor weeping like a spoiled baby. After a few moments of that she stands with a huge smile on her face. She kisses her hands and throws them to her fans in her head, looking all around. In her mind, she's just performed in front of thousands of people like the old days. All day, every day for the past twenty-two years in her mind she's been performing for her fans.

She takes a bow for her fans. Officer Jackson is so moved by her performance finds himself clapping out loud.

She looks over at him with shock. The look in her eyes makes him stop clapping. The cold and vicious look sends chills through his body. She stares through him for seconds causing the tension between them to build.

Not knowing what else to do, he looks away from her. He can feel her staring at him, but he tries to not look at her. Minutes go by and he peeks up only to find her at the gate in the exact same position. He looks at her and the exact same look is in her eyes. She stares at him without blinking.

Slowly her fierce look transpires into a bright and pleasant smile. She takes a bow to him as if all of that was just another part of her performance. He sits there confused as she takes off on her toes once again she starts on another ballot. Normally he peeks in at her ever so often but never has he watched her for this long of a period of time.

Her performance has left him wanting to watch more and more of her and he does. She dances for him for hours and hours without rest in between until his shift is over. His shift comes to an end, he claps and walks away from his desk. She continues on performing for the fans in her head.

Prison is her home, but performing is her life. Performing is the only thing that keeps her mind off of the fact that she's in prison. She's been dancing for her fans in her head for twenty-two years but to have a real audience tonight made all of her years of performing for those imaginary fans worth it. Those twenty-two years now feel like it was only rehearsal for the big show she had tonight. She's looking forward too many more shows for him.

Days Later...

It's 11:03 and instead of Officer Jackson being greeted by half naked women standing at their cell gates trying to entice him, the tier is chaotic. The alarm is sounding off and Correction Officers flood the center of the tier. It's apparent that a fight has broken out. Twenty Officers in riot gear stand in a huddle attempting to break up a fight while ten more come running in. The other inmates have been locked in. They stand at the gates cheering and inciting the riot.

He prepares himself mentally for all that's taking place. This is actually his first experience with this so he doesn't know exactly what to do so instead of rushing into the confusion, he stays back just watching it all. Once it seems to be somewhat diffused he starts to make his way over. Once the crowd opens up, he's quite surprised at what he sees.

It took five officers to restrain Naked Lucy. For the first time ever, her nudity is covered. She's dressed in a paper suit. Restraint doesn't seem to be necessary due to the fact that her hands are shackled in front of her. They're attempting to place her on the floor and shackle her ankles together, but she's putting up the fight of a lifetime.

Naked Lucy flips and flops sadistically with a demonic look in her eyes. The woman, Officer Jackson sees before his eyes right now, is not the woman he's been watching performing beautiful ballots. Thick foam drips from her mouth like a mad dog. She has a hatred for prison guards that one wouldn't believe. Each touch of one of them drives her even crazier and causes her to react like more of a mad woman.

As the five officers are trying their best to restrain her, three other officers wrestle with the little birthday girl from the other night. Two officers hold her down while the third one attempts to take the shank from her hand. She's crying like a baby in rage.

Dancing Lucy tries hard to get loose to get to the birthday girl. She looks up at the birthday girl who is now shank-less. Naked Lucy spits at the Birthday Girl causing the Birthday Girl to go almost insane. It takes more officers to get in between them. Naked Lucy shackled and helpless but the look in her eyes could kill. The look is arctic, freezing anything crosses in front of them. Three officers drag the young girl away.

As they near Officer Jackson, one of them whispers to him with evident sarcasm. "It's all your fault, Lover boy."

The officer exits the tier, leaving Officer Jackson baffled at his words. He walks over to the center where the officers are still trying to shackle Naked Lucy's feet. The more they try to restrain her, the unrulier she becomes. She kicks them with the strength of a mule, forcing them to the floor. She flips and flops like a fish out of water in order to prevent them from being able to shackle her.

The officers try hard to slam her onto her stomach to stop her from kicking. She spits in the face of one of the officers and he begins beating on her like a savage. She takes the abuse with ease. She smiles in his face with an evil grin as she takes his best shots. The look in her, yes is like that of a radical Black Panther.

"What the fuck is going on?" Officer Jackson asks the female officer who stands away from the action.

"You're what's going on."

"Me? What the fuck did I do?"

"It's a love triangle," she says with a smile.

"Huh?"

"Yeah, Officers Jones, Woods and Benson were escorting her to the nurse and the trustee came out of nowhere and jumped on her. Snuck her from behind and banged her across the back of the head with a lock in a sock. Knocked her to her knees. You see she had a knife too so she probably was gonna finish her off if she could."

"But where do I fit that picture?" he questioned with genuine uncertainty.

"The Trustee said something about she's trying to take her man from her." A huge smile spreads across her face.

"Her man?"

The woman officer nods her head up and down. Officer Jackson quickly replays the details of the last few nights. The Trustee's attempts to get his attention have been more relentless than ever. He even noticed a displeased look on her face as she stood before him and he couldn't keep his eyes off of the woman performing ballet in her cell.

He now realizes that this was all a lash out of her jealousy. It's hard for him to believe that she would act like this and how barely giving her conversation could lead her to believe that he's her man. In the real world, none of this makes sense but in prison, a place where the smallest thing is blown out of proportion to be the biggest thing it all makes perfect sense. In here, a place where these women have been forced to detach themselves from their children, loved ones and their most valuable possessions; the smallest of items are meaningful to them. Because they own nothing at all, any little thing, that they do own, means the world to them.

A person can lose their life over a magazine in this place. These women are territorial. They're little cramped up space is all they have. A kind word from a male officer could easily lead them to believe it's more being that some of them haven't had a kind word from a man in ages.

"The whole time that she was attacking the woman, all, she kept screaming, was, I was talking to him first." All of this sounds quite bizarre to him. "You be careful with these crazy women," she whispers.

His genuine concern kicks in. "What did she have to go the nurse for?"

"Probably dehydration as usual," the female officer replies.

"She dances day and the night non-stop while starving herself. She goes like that for months until she has to be hospitalized."

Naked Lucy's feet are finally shackled. She lays there still fighting as best she can. Officer Jackson looks over to her with compassion even though she's still reacting like a mad woman. The Lieutenant blows past them with fury pasted on his face.

"Take Lucifer to the hole!" he demands. Hearing those words ignites her to fight even harder through the shackles. The officers are still struggling gravely with her.

The female officer runs over to Naked Lucy's defense

"Lieutenant, it really wasn't her fault."

"I don't care! Take her to the hole!"

Officer Jackson now standing closer to Naked Lucy, watches her still in surprise. The officer mashes her face to the floor to prevent her from spitting in his face while another holds her legs together. Naked Lucy catches a glimpse of Officer Jackson in the midst of her struggle. She double takes. She stares at him and suddenly her fighting eases a little at a time until she no longer fights at all.

All the officers are now huffing and puffing while wondering what has come over her. Her whole demeanor has changed right before their very eyes and they don't have a clue as of why. She stares into Officer Jackson's eyes with a spark in her own eyes. Innocence slowly fills her eyes as a beautiful smile spreads across her face.

Two officers drag her onto her feet. She stands there with a pleasant look on her face as if she hasn't been giving them hell for the past twenty minutes. She doesn't blink as she looks at Officer Jackson with the googly eyes. She bats her long eyelashes at him as she blushes from ear to ear.

Everyone notices the change in her. They also realize that the change is all because of Officer Jackson. At this point, no one really cares why she's had the change of heart. They're just happy that she's calmed down.

"Take her to the hole!" the lieutenant demands once again. He storms off, exiting the tier.

The two officers push Naked Lucy into Officer Jackson's arms.

"Clean up your own mess," one officer whispers with rage.

Officer Jackson stands clueless for seconds as he holds Naked Lucy tight in his grip. She looks at him with the sweet googly eyes. Finally, he snatches her by the arm;

throwing her in front of him. He pushes her gently. All the inmates are screaming from their cells as they pass. Some are cheering for her and others are shouting hate against her. Naked Lucy stares straight ahead in her normal trance-like state.

Minutes later, Officer Jackson pushes Naked Lucy down the dark corridor of the dark and cold dungeon. Not a soul seems to be down here outside of them. The smell of death is in the air. The eerie feeling causes the hairs to stand up on his neck. He continues on, walking tall and confident. Jackson stands at the cell. He holds her by her handcuffs as he opens the cell. He pushes her inside and slams the gate quickly. Just as he was locking the gate, he gets caught by total surprise.

"Please don't leave these shackles on me," she begs.

For the first time, ever Naked Lucy speaks. It's reported that she hasn't said a word since she pleaded guilty to the murder charge twenty-two years ago. Jackson stares at her in shock. Her sweet baby voice is the total opposite of the mad woman he just saw a minute ago.

"I have to dance. If I can't dance, I will die. Dancing gives me life. With these shackles on, I can't dance."

Jackson stands in thought, not sure if he's supposed to leave the shackles on or not.

"Please?" she begs in an even sweeter voice.

"What's the worst that can happen," Jackson thinks to himself. *"She is the only one down here so who can she hurt?*

"Fuck it," he mumbled under his breath as he sticks the key into the lock.

He opens the cell and steps inside. He watches her closely. He examines her eyes, hoping to see any sign of that woman that he just watched for minutes take those officers through hell. The woman, he sees, is the dancer with the sweet baby voice.

Jackson kneels down slowly, never taking his eyes from hers. Slowly he reaches over to the shackles on her ankles. He opens the lock and stands on his feet quickly. Naked Lucy stares there with a look of innocence in her eyes.

"Turn around," Jackson instructs. She does as she's instructed to. She turns around, facing the wall. Jackson stands behind her with a half a foot in between them. He reaches in front of her and quickly unlocks the cuffs.

Before he can back away from her, a stiff elbow to the gut knocks the wind out of him.

"Agh!" he gasps as every bit of the air exits his body. The elbow to the gut transforms to a fist to the face. The impact of the punch sends Jackson crashing into the gate behind him.

Like a dangerous alley cat, Naked Lucy stands in front of him planning her attack.

"Meow!" she yells ferociously as she holds her hands in the air like paws.

Jackson is stuck on the gate, trying to shake away the dizziness from the blow, as well as refill the air in his lungs. Before he can get himself together she leaps at him like a cat. As she lands she digs her fingernails into his eyes, temporarily blinding him. He cries out from the pain.

He can't see a thing in front of him. Suddenly he hears the sound of the cuffs locking. His wrists are choked tightly with the metal cutting into his skin. He attempts to fight her off blindly, but he can't fight what he can't see. She taunts him, picking her shots at her own leisure.

He uses both hands to try and push her off. She falls backward on her butt. She becomes enraged. With no hesitation, she leaps at him like a cat once again. "Meow!."

She lands on top of him, her legs straddled over his thighs. He can't budge. His vision finally comes together and he's staring up at her. To his surprise there is the look of innocence in her eyes again. He's taken aback by her unpredictability. He watches with fear and suspense. He wants to bust a move, but he's in fear of her retaliation.

With the speed, so fast that he doesn't see it coming, she extends her face close to his. Her tongue slithers across his lips like a deadly snake. She locks onto his bottom lip and holds it tight as she runs her tongue over his bottom lip. He tries to squirm his way out of her grip, but she has him pinned to the floor. Her strength is no surprise to him after seeing her in action against the three officers.

She plants her kitten on top of his manhood, positioning it perfectly. She grinds on his manhood until it stiffens. She grinds so hard that the paper suit against his polyester trousers could set a fire. She grinds until her kitten moistens.

Twenty-two years of no male contact makes the kitten go from moist to soak and wet in seconds. In a matter of minutes, her juices have now soaked through the paper suit and even wet up his trousers. She continues to grind, driving him sexually insane. The thought of fighting her off is not even an afterthought at this time.

The only thing on his mind is trying to aim the head of his dick perfectly and driving it right through the paper suit that she's wearing. As he concentrates on that, Naked Lucy slides her pussy up and down his shaft. She closes her eyes and allows her imagination to take over. She pictures his dick trapped in the tight trousers, begging to be freed.

The more her imagination takes over the wetter her pussy gets. She can envision his dick clearly. As she slides over the shaft, she can feel his thickness. Her lips spread wide and wrap around his thickness. She slows up her pace allowing her clit to float over the thick vein in the middle of his shaft.

She slides her pussy up and down his shaft, teasing the hole after every long slide. She grinds circles on the shaft before sliding along it at rapid speed. Her clit bounces over the vein like a speed bump. Her clit lands on the head of his dick, bouncing two or three times before sitting flush on the tip.

She can feel the head of his dick pulsating, swelling and becoming fatter and fatter with each breath. She positions her clit right on top of the protruding vein and leaves it there. She can feel the blood rushing through his dick at a rapid pace. The heavy flow tickles her clit, causing it to stand up at attention. Her clit trembles with horniness.

She snatches the paper suit open, giving him an up close view of her beautiful breasts. He stares at them in awe. Her stiffened nipples stare at him, begging to be touched. She grabs his hands and places them on her breast. He immediately begins exploring them.

He flicks her nipples with his thumbs as he caresses her breast. She arches her back and leans her head back. Moans of ecstasy escape her lips. She leans forward, her breast cupped in her hands. She feeds them to him.

He licks, sucks and slurps on her nipple as she teases his lips with it. The teasing turned her on so immensely that she shoves the whole tit into his mouth. As his mouth is filled with her tit, he tongue kisses the nipple, allowing his tongue to twirl around it freely.

She shoves both tits into his mouth and he lets his tongue bounce from nipple to nipple, back and forth. As he feasts on her tits, she grinds away on him until her pussy is a puddle of hot sexual juices. She lifts up of off him with no warning. He looks up at her in suspense as she snatches the paper suit off of her. Her naked body is like a work of art to him.

She stands over him dancing elegantly, allowing him to appreciate her body. Her performance turns her on more than it turns him on. Her pussy heats up until she can no longer bear the heat. She's scorching and needs the fire put out.

She dives onto him, pussy to his mouth. No need for instructions because he knows exactly what she needs. She slides her lips over his. He uses his tongue to find her love button. He flicks the clit with his tongue until it stands erect for him.

He places a kiss on it before sucking it gently. Her body jolts with satisfaction. She arches her back, sliding her button up and down his tongue like a sliding board. She reaches behind and fumbles with the zipper of his trousers until she's located her prize. She rubs her fingers over the head teasingly as he now teases her hole with the tip of his tongue.

He stops teasing long enough to plant a kiss on the hole. He licks around the hole before driving the tip of his tongue inside. Slowly, he begins to tongue fuck her. His stiffened tongue slides in and out slowly. The tip of his tongue strokes her g-spot causing her body to tremble with every stroke.

She grabs the back of his head as she force feeds the pussy to him. She pumps his mouth erratically. He attempts to pull away to catch his breath in order not to suffocate, but she holds his head that much tighter. He looks up at her helplessly as her face displays the cold look that he fears.

Her eyes fierce and vicious lets him know that she's no longer the innocent dancer and has become the mad murderer once again. Unsuspectedly, she hauls off and slaps him silly. Before he can absorb that blow she sends another his way and another and another.

Abusing him turns her on. She backhands him before face-masking him. She palm-grips his face, smothering him as he tries to fight her off. Finally, she gives in and plants her pussy on his face once again. She suffocates his mouth with her wet pussy. She fights back the urge to orgasm. She stops in order to regain her control.

She smears sweet pussy juice over his lips, beard, nose, eyes. His face is now a sticky mess and he loves it. She leans over and kisses him passionately. The taste of her own pussy excites her. She licks the remaining juices off of his lips, careful not to miss a single drop.

A sudden movement causes his eyes to pop open. He watches as she changes position. Her ass bent over his face is the most beautiful sight. He uses his cuffed hands to spread her ass wide. He dives in face first and eats her from behind. She backs it up on his tongue, signaling him to stick the tongue inside and he does.

She uses both hands to stroke his enormous penis. One hand on the shaft and the other on the head, she jerks him slowly. Rotating her hands counterclockwise gets the reaction that she's looking for. His rod stiffens as juice seeps from the head.

She places her lips on the head in order not to waste his juices. She sucks the head, draining the juice from it. Her mouth is quickly filled with syrup. His head swells and contracts indicating that he's ready to bust. It's been twenty-two long years and she refuses to waste a rock hard erection.

She bunny hops off him, landing right on his manhood. She doesn't waste a second before bouncing up and down on it like a trampoline. Their moans echo throughout the dungeon loudly as she fucks away twenty-two years of sexual frustration.

She can feel the head swelling inside of her. He paints her walls with the head of his dick as he spreads her cheeks wider and wider. She holds her breath as he goes deeper than anyone has ever gone. She gasps for air as he slow dicks her down deeper and deeper.

With no warning at all, he fills her up with hot lava. His juices splatter against her walls causing her to cream at the very same time. The both of them sit still as their juices marinate together. She collapses face in between his feet with no energy nor life left inside of her. Twenty-two years of buildup has been released and it was well worth the wait. He manages to catch a glimpse of her sleeping body before he falls asleep as well.

90 Minutes Later....

What seemed like an eternity was only the passing of ninety minutes when Officer Jackson opened his eyes. He was lying on the ground, the cuffs were neatly placed back on his belt and Naked Lucy was in the corner again dancing for a crowd. She barely made eye contact with him and he was a bit relieved but at the same time curious as to why she was back to her zombie trance-like state that had many questioning her sanity.

Officer Jackson didn't want to lose his job but what had transpired between the two had left him with a lasting impression, quite similar to her ballet moves she often entertained him with. He got up off the floor and immediately greeted with the pounding of a headache, but he did not let that distract him. He fixed his uniform, gained his composure and exited the cell. As he removed the key from the lock he looked once over at her and there she was dancing to the beat of her own drum and totally unbothered by his presence or his luring eye. He blinked several times before walking down the hall back to the tier, still a bit perplexed by what had taken place...

THE END OR IS THIS JUST THE BEGINNING...

A MOTHER SCORNED
By Unique Penn

The first one had been the hardest. But after months of mental and physical preparation, intricate planning, and an endless supply of anger; Veronica had finally fulfilled her destiny. She left behind the grieving mother she had been to become the vigilante for justice she needed to be. The first time she had pulled the trigger, there had been a moment of hesitation. She had almost lost the nerve to do what needed to be done; like so many other black folks in history. It was not until she looked into the soulless eyes of her son's killer that her anxiety swiftly disappeared and she pulled the trigger.

The silencer on Veronica's gun ensured that no one would hear the deadly shots. And the fact she had lured him into an area devoid of video cameras insured her anonymity. Veronica knew she would be caught eventually; all serial killers usually were. Especially, high profile killers such as she. She did not consider herself a serial killer, but the media was comparing her to a new age racialized Dexter. She hated that reference but it did not matter. Since her son Dante's life had been taken she felt she had nothing to lose.

There had been seven others since the first time Veronica pulled the trigger. Some had been men, some women but the one commonality they held was the fact they were all police officers who murdered unarmed black citizens. Each and every one had been exonerated or acquitted of their crimes of murdering black men, women and children. And each time Veronica's heart broke. Not only had the murderers been exonerated, they had gained notoriety and small amounts of wealth from their evil deeds.

Paid murderers is what they were. Much like the overseers and patty rollers during slavery times. They were paid to keep black people in their designated place and championed for slaughtering those who failed to comply. Since its inception America had yet to outlaw the lynching of black citizens, despite the fact slavery had come to an end over a hundred years ago. Veronica had cried with the mothers of Trayvon and Tamir. And, watched in sadness and horror as the wife of Eric Garner and family of Freddie Grey were forced to watch the murderers of their loved ones go free.

Veronica had watched the suspicious suicide of Sandra Bland unfold on the news and social media, and couldn't help but to think how that could have been her. But, it was not until she watched the death of her sixteen-year old son being gunned down by a police officer; did the feeling truly hit home. After a while, she found that she could no longer cry for those mothers. She was too busy crying for herself. She had cried for months. Every waking hour was filled with tears until it seemed her eyes were permanently blood shot and swollen.

When the crying became too much, Veronica she began to spend more hours sleeping than she was awake. She experienced deep sleep with vivid dreams of her baby boy during happier times. It was these dreams that caused her to sleep sixteen hours out of the day. She did not want to wake up because she did not want to let go of her son. Who had become a reality while she slept. She was depressed and all her dreams and hopes for the future had died with Dante. In a sense Veronica had died with her son. And nothing brought her more pleasure than seeing his smiling face. She could care less that her eyes had to be closed for this to be accomplished.

One night, Veronica had been forced out of a deep sleep and blissful dream by the call of her bladder. She bid her son farewell for a few moments and relieved herself. She went into the kitchen and poured herself a glass of wine before settling on the couch to watch her son be murdered once again. She lit the blunt of loud she had been smoking prior to her previous beauty rest. This was part of her self-medicating ritual to induce long periods of sleep. Veronica tuned into the television and watched her world unravel for the millionth time.

She watched as Dante obediently follow the officer's orders and step out of the car. She cringed every time she saw the cream colored Lexus. She was sure that was the reason her son had been pulled over in the incident leading to his murder. It was the first and unfortunately the only time he had ever driven her brand new car. He had begged her for months leading up to the Big Sean concert she had brought him tickets for. They were supposed to be a reward for him being the valedictorian of his graduating class. He was trying to impress his date and had finally worn her down.

The laundry list of do's and don'ts in her vehicle didn't dim his excitement one bit. As he had answered, "Yes ma'am" to all her demands. When he left their home that fateful night, he had been smiling. The next time Veronica saw her child, he was dead.

Without warning, Dante reached in his back pocket for his wallet and his body jumped in response to a barrage of bullets that drained the life from his body. The thirteen bullets that tore through his innocent flesh stained his yellow Polo shirt a dark purple. His almost lifeless body slumped against the brand new Lexis as he fought for his last breath. Veronica swallowed the last of her wine in one gulp and refused to cry another tear.

As she watched her sons date exit the passenger side of the car in a flurry of blond hair and fair skin, the tears threatened to fall. She swallowed them down as she inhaled smoke from her swisher and watched the rest unfold. In shock and anger she ignored the police officers' warnings to step away from her dying companion. Although there was no audio, the exchange of body language spoke volumes as the officer holstered his gun and tazed the distraught girl. She had held firm to Dante's almost lifeless body as she screamed and kicked at the officer who had shot him. He claimed he needed to taze her to get her under control. Veronica watched as she lie awkwardly twitching slumped over Dante's dead body.

Veronica restarted the video and went to refill her glass.

"Momma."

That voice. Was it all in her head or was she in another dream and he was really here in the deepest part of her imagination? This had become her waking routine. Drink, smoke, watch that video and maybe eat. She had shed fifteen pounds from her already slight frame since his death. She ignored what she assumed she heard and tossed the empty bottle in the trash. She pressed play on her remote, but stared experiencing technical difficulties.

"Momma."

There was that voice again and suddenly for the first time in months, Veronica no longer felt alone. As if the invisible atoms in the air were miraculously formed into a semi solid state of her deceased son; Dante now stood in front of her television in that same yellow shirt with the blood stains. Veronica didn't know what to make of this moment. In a gesture of nervousness, she picked up her glass and began to take gulp.

Veronica reached out to touch her son and for a brief moment he was flesh and blood in reality where things like that were not possible. For months now she had watched that video over and over, praying that God would allow her one more chance to hold her baby. Now Veronica knew that she was not alone. God had carried her this far and had no intentions on leaving her side. But as soon as she connected with her sons image it disappeared.

"I'm so sorry baby boy. I shouldn't have let you drive that car."

Veronica had felt guilt since Dante's murder. Although she had tried to shield him from the evils of the world, a young black man driving an expensive car raised the odds of racial profiling taking place. She never thought her son would be victimized in such a manner. Thoughts of Dante growing and blossoming into an articulate, respectful, intelligent young man had enticed Veronica into buying stock in the American dream, in recent months she realized that dream was the biggest Ponzi scheme in history.

Before his life was stolen he was preparing for graduation. He was valedictorian and the new, freshly pressed cap and gown that he would never get to wear still hung on the back of his bedroom door. Always a constant reminder of what could have been. Should have been; and what now needed to be. Veronica felt a lump forming in the back of her throat, she forced it down with a swallow of wine and willed herself to not shed another tear. In the end the wine, weed, and pain won out and Veronica cried herself to sleep once again with the death of her son on replay.

Veronica was in her favorite place with her favorite person. Her subconscious replaying all the memories that she shared with her son while she slept. Tonight, they were on the swings in Palmer Park. It was in their old neighborhood and held good and bad memories for her. This was the place she shared some of the first memories in Dante's subconscious. This was also the place where his father was gunned down when he was three. Veronica hadn't physically been to the park or the old neighborhood since then, but for some reason it seemed to be a reoccurring setting in her dreams.

"Momma. Don't look so sad."

Dante held her hand as the two swung in unison.

"I'm not sad when I am here with you" Veronica squeezed his hand tighter in the only world she could still touch him physically.

"Momma, you know this place is not real right? You do realize you're not really holding my hand?" Dante said in response to Veronica's hold on his hand.

"Hush Dante..." Veronica attempted to scold him, but he cut her off.

"You got to let me go Momma. I'm good trust me." Dante smiled and his deep dimples melted her heart.

"I can't let you go. What do I have without you?" With each passing moment Dante grew more faint.

"Look ma, after tonight I can't visit you anymore. You do not belong in this purgatory waiting for me. You should be amongst the living."

Tears sprang from Veronica's eyes as she shook her head at her son's request. Dante leaned over, kiss his mother's forehead and vanished from her dream. Instantly Veronica awakened from her slumber. Her face was wet with tears as she thought of how Dante would not be returning. Out of habit Veronica reached for her glass and when she found it empty she threw it against the wall and watched it shatter. In that moment something snapped inside of her.

In that moment Veronica knew what must be done. She would take her sons advice and return to the world of the living. Veronica had been baptized by the flames of hell but when she returned she was not the grieving mother that had found peace in dreamland. She was now a warrior. Clothed in the armor of God and armed with a sword of vengeance from Satan's lair, Veronica was ready to show the world the Hell had no fury like a mother's scorn.

That night Veronica began the mental and physical training she would need to avenge her son's death. Every time she wanted to give up, she went into her son's room and looked at the unworn graduation gown and her anger grew. When her arms got tired from holding a gun for hours straight at the gun range, she thought of all the black mother's across America in her position. Mother's like herself who were paralyzed with grief and numbness as they tried to move on with their lives.

But that is where the comparisons ended. Unlike those other mothers who were able to go on national television and forgive their child's murder and ignore the blank racism in their face, she had refused. No press conferences, no television or radio appearances for her. When the city threatened to explode in rioting due to Dante's death, the black community took her silence as the thumbs up to burn the city down.

The media even had the audacity to attack her character saying she should ask the people to stop the violence. Who the hell did they think she was? Rodney King? Fuck peace. Where were these same people while her son was being gunned down by the boys in blue? Political correctness and generational conditioning of the descendants of slaves dictated she was supposed to forgive and pray for peace. As far as she was concerned, there could be no peace until the racist psychopaths were put down like the rabid dogs they were.

The police were the largest terrorist organization in America and their actions were being approved by local and federal governments, by their inaction to prosecute or even fire the reckless police officers. And since it seemed no one truly had the balls to stand up to the establishment, it was up to Veronica. Her brand of justice did not require marches and sit ins. Her brand of justice required bullets and blood, the only language white folk understood was money and war. And if they wanted a war she would definitely give them one.

Black lives mattered to Veronica. Especially the life of her son. She would be the first to demonstrate exactly how true that statement was. She might be the last, but what did she have to lose. They had already taken her greatest treasure.

The first time she pulled the trigger had been the hardest. The rest had been easy. Each time she sent one of the demons back to hell, she left a picture of a black face who was slain by the police. She made sure to leave the photo of the child each officer had slain so that the world would know why they had been killed. The police were able to keep these incidents undercover until one of the media outlets caught on to the serial killings and caused panic amongst white communities.

While the police were scrambling for leads and suspects, the public was scrambling for guns and ammunition. All it had taken was a video clip of black citizen in line to purchase guns and conceal and carry permits for panic to set in. America's biggest fear had come to fruition, an armed black assailant hell bent on destroying the oppressive institutions the supported America's brand of democracy.

Law enforcement was at a loss as to who had the audacity to attack the police with no remorse. FBI profilers were brought on in attempts to construct a physical and mental picture of the perpetrator who they assumed was a disgruntled white male in his late thirties. Not one of the idiots had the gumption to believe that a person of color could be capable of something like this. Black folks could never be as calculating, ruthless, and intelligent enough to pull this off. So while they continued to look for a white man, a black woman continued to dole out her own brand of justice.

The media and social networks had dubbed her, #Black Justice and her exploits were trending topics throughout the net. Veronica had singlehandedly created fear and panic in the hearts of white America. Black bloggers and columnist compared her to a modern day Nat Turner while the hoods began to come off America's closeted racist. Politics and race were being debated in the workplace, social media and public settings. Tensions ran high amongst the races but that was nothing new.

Everyone had their opinion but only one opinion seemed to matter and that was hers. The only dark cloud was the increasing police presence in black communities were they were made to feel like prisoners in their own homes. City wide curfews were enforced as a race war brewed in the streets of America. Veronica was a hero in the black community and a scourge to the whites. Those who championed her cause took to posting the names of officers they believed should be added to the kill list.

She had been able to carry on with her brand of justice for weeks before the authorities were able to catch up with her. Veronica had grown bold in her brand of vengeance and found herself checking g the list of names she gathered from the Internet. The name that kept ringing every bell was the infamous George Zimmerman. Her first mind told her was to high profile and loved attention. Catching him off guard might be difficult. But the more she thought about it, Veronica started to see that had it not been for George Zimmerman open season on young black men in the new millennium might not have been opened.

This asshole had become the poster boy for racism in America. He had shown that it was still socially acceptable and legal to take a black life. There would be no repercussions only rewards for your actions. Zimmerman had made a small fortune off of the murder of Trayvon. He had lynched that baby and the legal system upheld his actions. Veronica disagreed. It was time someone showed George the rope swung both ways.

When it hit the grapevine that George Zimmerman lifeless body had been found on the side of a deserted Florida highway, the Internet broke. Over a billion views of videos related to his murder brought out the worst in some Americans. Black America were celebrating like Obama had won a third term in office as they celebrated in the streets. Meme's that featured his lifeless body flooded black twitter and fb. While racist rednecks were chugging liquid courage and loading their shot guns preparing for war.

But it was at that very crime scene that Veronica made her mistake. She caught him stumbling drunk as he left some honky tonk bar in the middle of nowhere. When she saw his car pull out the parking lot she pulled out from her hiding placed followed him with her lights out until she was a safe distance from civilization. Veronica placed her police lights in her front window, signaling George to pull over.

He pulled over highly intoxicated, but not worried about police contact. He had been through this drill numerous times and he had yet to suffer for any of his transgressions.

Veronica approached his vehicle. She was dressed in her freshly pressed uniform and her shiny badge displaying her city and badge number flashed in the night. Ironically, this uniform the one she had worn every day to work for over ten years that aided her in disarming her victims; was the same uniform Dante's killer wore to work.

Her black fact blended into the blue uniform just enough to disguise her true intentions and take the lives of those most deserving. And George was at the top of her list.

"License and registration." Veronica demanded in that no nonsense police voice she had been taught to use.

"Was I speeding officer?" was the reply as George handed over his registration and license.

Ignoring him she continued.

"Are there any weapons or drugs in your possession?"

"Yes, I have a registered gun in the glove box and my conceal and carry permit is right next to it."

Bingo! That's what Veronica was waiting for.

"Please step out of the car sir."

He complied knowing that he could get a DUI if she chose to charge him with one. Veronica went directly to the glove box and removed the Holy grail of new age lynching. The gun that had taken the life of Trayvon Martin. She checked the gun found that it was fully loaded with the safety off. This fool was always ready to take a life. He was a menace to society and he needed to be stopped. In that moment a surge of anger coursed through Veronica's veins as she split his head open with the button of the gun.

"What the fuck?" George screamed in surprise and pain as he stumbled backwards grabbing his wound that was gushing blood.

Before he could gain his balance, Veronica silenced him with an expert chop to the throat that caused him to fall to the ground. She viciously kicked him in the balls with her steel toed boots and Zimmerman quickly found out he could not nurse his injuries as fast as she was delivering the blows. Veronica felt ending his life quickly with a bullet would have shown too much mercy. So instead she began to beat and kick him within an inch of his life.

She kicked him so hard with so much force that his testicles were literally crushed and had exploded inside his body, according to the coroner's report. She made sure to kick him for every one of the thirteen bullets that pierced her sons flesh. She kicked him for every bullet lodged in Trayvon's chest and for every lie he had told. As her boot smashed into his septum, she made sure to kick him with the force of the feet of a million slaves running towards freedom. When she was done kicking him, he was a bloody pulp on the side of a lonely highway.

Although he was already dead, veronica could not resist the urge to put a bullet in his chest from the same gun, in the same manner he had killed Trayvon. She placed a picture of Trayvon smiling face on the bloody corpse of George Zimmerman and drove off into the night.

Veronica had left the majority of her hurt, frustration and anger in the lifeless body of a child killer. She had meant to rid herself of it all but a small amount still remained for the man responsible for her child's death. The thought of Dante caused her to reach for her breast pocket, where she always kept his photo to settle her aching heart and frazzled nerves. She found it gone. Unfortunately, Veronica had left that picture alongside side of the road with all her pain. That picture would be her undoing.

Her prints were found all over the photograph of Dante. When the police showed up at her door to arrest her, she went without incident, but remained tight lipped throughout their interrogation. Once she opened her mouth and invoked her right to remain silent, the shit hit the fan and racial lines were drawn in the streets. Racial skirmishes sprung up across the country and in the eyes of white's veronica was to blame. In the eyes of blacks, it was what needed to happen. Maybe the police would think twice before pulling the trigger.

One of their own had made them targets after her the life of her child had been snatched from the land of the living. A nation was finally forced to address racism and the institutions that continued to perpetuate its principles. Veronica had no problem sitting in a cell she had sent many to awaiting her fate. The only crime she had committed was being black and unable to protect what was rightfully yours.

While the grand jury sat debating the validity of her indictment, a nation of black citizens stood in solidarity against police brutality and the slick ways the government were stripping citizens of their constitutional rights outside the courthouse. In the middle stood police in riot gear trying to separate the growing crowd of supporters and protesters.

The lines would not hold much longer as anxiety and tensions grew amongst those waiting for the grand jury decision. The panel of all white jurors decided to charge Veronica with seven counts of first degree murder. Veronica defense lawyer quickly stated they would be entering a not guilty plea, by reason of insanity. He wished her well before she was led back to her cell.

That night veronica slept better than she had in months. Gone were the feelings of fear, worry, regret, helplessness. She knew she had done everything she could to ensure that she found justice for her son and all those other countless black face forgotten in the annals of American history. For the first time she knew that the death of an innocent black child had not been in vain. She had struck a blow for justice, democracy, and black folks in one strike. America had finally learned hell had no fury like a black mother scorned.

THE LYING KING

By Justin Q Young & Imani Ferrier

Harmony

Put your arms around me boy; I got something to show you...
Keri Hilson's smooth melodic voice serenaded me from the Bose speakers on my dresser. The lights were dim and the mood was set, thanks to the accompaniment of the song. I laid on the silk sheets of my king sized bed and rubbed my hands over my thighs. I was turned on; turned on by the effects of the wine that was kicking in, and turned on by the thoughts of Quincy. My addiction to orgasms was scary.

I couldn't survive without feeling that release at least three times a day. Some people would call me an addict, but on the contrary, I was addicted to the pleasure. I was addicted to the surge that ran through my body right before my legs began to convulse, and my blood pressure rose. I was addicted to the crippling feeling, and the way my lower back would arch when I finally let go. I needed to feel that deep penetration, flesh against flesh. It's something about the heat of a man that can take you places you just can't go with a toy.

At the moment I settled, I pulled my silver bullet out of the top drawer of my night stand, excited about the feeling I was about to have. I called it Mad Max, not for any particular reason, just a name I came up with randomly. I powered it up and gently placed it on the middle of my love button. My breathing increased as the pulsation I felt against my wet clitoris was invigorating and made my eyes close for a second and feel goose bumps rising up on my arms and legs. This was a feeling that was euphoric and one that I chased repeatedly.

Briefly, I had noticed the steam from the shower I started to prepare was beginning to fog up the bathroom mirror and slowly was lingering out into the bedroom. I made no attempt to adjust it, instead I turned my head into the pillow and lost myself in the moment. I bit down on my lower lip as my legs began to shake and I felt my thighs tightening up on me. This was the ultimate feeling as I could envision Quincy's tall chocolate muscular body flexing as we had intercourse. Visions of him flooded my mind as my fingers began going into overdrive inside of my sweet wet garden.

I imagined seeing Quincy on top of me, looking down and watching my facial expressions as he slowly and deeply penetrated. I was turned on and in the moment, so much so that I applied a finger from my wetness and placed it inside of my warm mouth tasting the pure sweetness of my arousal. I imagined his fingers being the ones I was sucking, caressing my body, and handling my petite frame. As I increased the speed of the bullet, I increased the rhythm of my body grinding my hips to the baseline of the song.

Talking with my fingertips, I've got so much to say babe; let's see can you read my hips...

With the fingertips on my right hand, I traced circles around my nipples and continued this private dance. In my mind, Mad Max wasn't satisfying my appetite, Quincy was. I imagined him penetrating me deeply while staring at my body with his deep set almond shaped bedroom eyes. He would start off slowly, but increase his pace as the tempo to the song sped up. At every crescendo I would moan, and at ever decrescendo, his soft baritone voice would hum in my ear. I bit my bottom lip as I dipped my fingertip inside of my wetness and brought my finger up to my mouth. I licked the juices off and traced that hand back down my thighs. Keri Hilson's octaves were causing my body to move in ways I hadn't known them to move before.

I put Max on his highest speed and traced the walls of my pussy. With his help, Quincy almost had me on the verge of climaxing. I imagined this man turning me on my stomach and penetrating me from behind; my soft backside pressed against his tight mid-section as we rocked together to the beat.

Read between the lines, as we bump and grind; trust me, it feels better from behind, so one more time...

At that point, I didn't know whether to call out Max's name, Quincy's name, or Keri's name. My body was on fire, and it needed to be extinguished. My legs were bent at the knee in the air as I laid on my stomach with the bullet pressed hard against my clitoris. I was dripping wet, and the sound of the vibrator gently humming against the juices flowing from my pussy was driving me crazy. I was ready to cum; ready to send my body free falling off the cliff that I was teetering on.

I imagined Quincy raking his fingers down my back as he grabbed my hair and roughly pulled me back against him. He wanted me; needed me to cum so he could see that he satisfied me. The deep growls emerging from the pit of his stomach told me he was ready to release as well. I inserted Max all the way inside of me and traced my walls in a circular motion gripping my sheets with my other hand as my face lay buried within the pillows of my bed. I screamed out in pleasure as Max continued to hit my spot. My back stiffened up, my thighs began to shake, and I squeezed my eyes shut so tight, I could see stars. I began to shiver and shake from his slow and steady strokes.

Make this moment last forever babe; your body's calling me...

"Yes baby! Yes! I feel it cumming daddy! Ooh, Quincy I need you baby. Harder. Harder. Harder!" I screamed at the top of my lungs.

Keri Hilson hit her last high note, and just like that it was over. I opened my eyes and tried to control my breathing. I was all of out of breath, and my thighs were sticky from my sweetness dripping from my honeypot. That felt so real.

Quincy took me to new heights; took me to the moon and the stars, a place I had never been before. This feeling was almost indescribable. I never knew there was someone out there who could ever have the ability mentally to pleasure me more than myself or Max, but Quincy did. He awakened something inside of me; something I didn't think existed. He showed me that men are capable of committing themselves to lovemaking just as much as women are. This man did more than make love to me, he took me mentally to a place I had hidden even from myself. After being broken repeatedly by other guys before him, I was guarded.

The single act of having him look at me completely naked, whole and without judgment for what seemed like an eternity before he even made love to me, touched me in a way I couldn't put into words. I can't really explain what the fuck this man did to me but I've been seeing him whenever I closed my eyes, when I drive to work, and when I dream resting my eyes at night. A few moments ago I was screaming his name as I pleasured myself with Max. I had it bad, thoughts of us meeting that first time flooded my memory. I couldn't believe that this man and I had made love within thirty minutes of our meeting; his touch hasn't left my body. His embrace is unforgettable. The way our bodies intertwined with one another you would've thought we were one in the same.

At the time when I met him, I was going through some major changes in my life, and wasn't ready to make the type of commitment that being in a relationship required. I was living in the moment and getting into a committed relationship I felt would only complicate things. I enjoyed the moments Quincy and I shared together, they played and replayed in my head. Due to all of the heartbreak I had endured in my life, I was emotionally unstable and my heart was unavailable to anyone but myself. Meeting Quincy wasn't a part of my plan, he caught me off guard. My behavior that day didn't surprised me, being as impulsive as I was but what occurred thereafter has been.

Normally it's just about the sex for me, nothing more nothing less. Mentally I have protected myself by going into situations with the frame of mind of not having expectations, that way I don't get hurt when these little boys pretending that they are men come with the bitchassness. No strings attached is my motto. Quincy however, he wouldn't just accept the sex. He sees in me so much more than I see in myself and I question at times if I can live up to what he wants from me.

All I've had is pain and feel I'm incapable of loving anyone other than myself. These are the types of thoughts that I have in my head as I further think about him, us, and this situation. He believes he can show me differently, yet we are creatures of habit.

"Hey baby what's on your mind? You've been quiet the entire date. Is everything ok?

"Everything is fine Kendall. I'm just a little tired. I guess that shower drained me." I lied.

Of course I wasn't fine; the date was going terribly wrong. Don't get me wrong Kendall is sweet and charming. Women pray for men like him, but that's just the thing, I'm not your ordinary woman. Kendall is a boring man who prefers staying at home and cuddling under the soft glow of the fireplace, rather than going out to a dinner and a comedy show. He'd rather spend his Saturday nights curled up on my leather sectional than out bowling or hitting up a nightclub. Most women would love a man like that but I'm young and vivacious, and don't see that type of life with him.

"Baby, I'm sorry. I'm really not feeling too well. Can you have the waitress bring the check. Dinner will be on me since I'm ending early."

"Harmony don't be silly and don't ever insult me like that again. It's not your fault you're feeling ill. I'll bring you home and rub you down until you fall asleep if that's ok with you?"

"Aww Kendall, you're far too kind. But, I'm sure that I will be just fine sweetie. I really think I may be coming down with the bug and we don't need you catching that now, do we?" I countered, rubbing his hand with mines for a dramatic effect.

I was hoping that he got the fucking clue that I didn't want to be bothered anymore for the evening. Call me a bitch, stuck up or whatever but this nigga just didn't move my bones.

"Ok, Harmony you're right. You'll need your beauty rest and I have a lot of work that needs to be completed. At least let me run you to the local pharmacy to get you some meds. I'd feel better knowing I was able to do something to help you feel better baby."

"Ok sweetie that's fine. I just feel so weak and I really need to rest. I promise I'll call you in the morning." I lied while wiping my face with the cloth that was on the table.

I was really putting on an Oscar winning performance to get out of that restaurant. I didn't need to waste any more time. Kendall is persistent but not as aggressive as I like, he's sexy but doesn't have the type of swag I desire, however for the meantime, I'm just going through the motions. Now -a-days you can't trust these dudes so you gotta keep a backup in the event one falls short, you will always bounce back with another.

Kendall did exactly as he said. He paid for dinner and took me to Walgreens. The drive home was quiet and awkward. I think Kendall wanted to speak but didn't know what to say. Another reason why I couldn't logically see myself spending forever with him was because I needed a man that could take charge tell me what to do; rough me up but not too much, but just enough to keep me in line. I need enough to make me want you and only you, I didn't want to ever crave another man's touch or voice. I only want eyes for one guy.

Unfortunately, Kendall isn't anywhere near my level. He practically carried me to my freaking doorstep.

"Hold on Harmony, let me get the door for you." Kendall rushed to my side of the car smiling. I exhaled deeply and rubbed the bridge of my nose. This poor guy is too sweet for his own good. My thoughts went back to Quincy, was he really that one for me.

"I really hate that you're feeling so bad baby," he said to me.

"Me too bae. I'll call you tomorrow okay?"

"Okay. Goodnight beautiful. Sleep tight."

He wrapped me up in his arms and kissed my forehead.

"Goodnight, Kendall."

I closed the door behind me and thought 'good riddance.'

****

Quincy

I knew the moment she caught my eye, that my life could change. This lady had the look I envisioned in my dreams that my wife would have, and I just knew I wanted her. It was something unexplainable, a connection I was drawn to. I watched for a moment as she fumbled with the bracelets on her wrist, looking at how she crossed her legs at the ankles, waiting patiently with her bags beside her. Her legs were thick just as her thighs were and I imagined what she was sitting on looked just as pretty.

The hair I figured was an expensive weave, maybe that Cambodian Kinky Curly or Mongolian Curly that the women were raving about on my Instagram timeline. I smiled at the thought, throwing my duffel bag on my shoulder, that I was remembering names to weaves. How crazy was it, I thought, as I shook my head and proceeded to walk towards my destiny.

I wondered the purpose of her travel, a photo shoot, job opportunity or maybe some sort of conference brought her into town. So many random thoughts swam around my head as I looked over in her direction periodically, stealing glimpses of her while waiting in line to be helped. This woman's caramel complexion was talking to me. I could imagine vividly, kissing every little spot on her body as if we had had sex already.

As I headed to the counter to check in, to my surprise; I found out that the reservations I made with Hotwire online hadn't been processed.

"What do you mean, I have a reservation number and everything that Hotwire emailed."

I opened the paper I had printed out, placed it on the counter to show the clerk.

"I apologize for the inconvenience sir but the credit card information that they use to pay us, hasn't cleared. This isn't your fault and it doesn't happen often but I trust it shouldn't take long before things get straight."

"So what do you suggest that I do?" I asked feeling frustrated.

"If you have a seat over in this area, I will personally make sure you are taken care of." The clerk assured all with a smile on her face. I couldn't complain knowing that the area she was referring to, was where Miss Beautiful was at.

I walked over by the couches and placed my bags on the floor.

"You get caught up in the bullshit with Hotwire too?" I questioned.

She looked up and shook her head in disgust. "Yes and this don't make no damn sense."

I couldn't make out her accent but it was sexy. My eyes honed in on her lips, the fullness of them. I felt like a snake being charmed by the flute of a snake charmer.

"I'm, Quincy. So, how long have you been waiting?" I extended my hand to meet her.

"Close to twenty minutes. My name is Harmony." Her touch was electric.

Our eyes lingered on one another, having conversations that our tongues hadn't formulated the words to say.

"Excuse me Ms. Francis, I have your accommodations ready." The hotel clerk interrupted

We both stood transfixed another moment before releasing each other. Harmony smiled, as did I. She bent to get her bags and walked back to the counter. Of course I watched the way her ass seemed to dance to its own beat.

"Damn, I know she got some good pussy." I whispered to myself.

I wasn't seated long before I received a text message from a lady friend back home I was dealing with. When I saw her name come across the screen, I exhaled because I was reminded about how things in our lives come to us for a purpose, a reason or a season. This particular relationship had run its course I felt and though I had made it clear I wanted a little distance, she refused to accept things.

"It's hard to let go of something you really want. I don't want to lose you, Quincy"

I shook my head, knowing the real reason why she wanted me around was because of what I could do for her. It's funny how women think they are using a man.

I exited the text and hit delete, looked up over at Harmony heading to the elevator and made the most impulsive decision I have ever made.

Quickly gathering my things, I headed in the direction I'd seen her go.

"Harmony?" she turned to face me.

"I was hoping you would stop me." she responded as the doors pinged open.

We both entered inside and without hesitation I reached out and grabbed this woman as if she belonged to me. Her bag dropped off of her shoulder, hitting the floor as she let out a moan when our lips touched each other for the first time.

Harmony pressed her body against mines and I explored her every curve with my hands; feeling how soft she felt to my touch. Our tongues played with one another as I bent her head slightly, to kiss her neck. I knew that was her spot as her body became more relaxed within my arms.

The elevator slowing down and making the pinging sound, alerted us that the doors were about to open. When they did a young man had taken a step to enter but seeing the looks on both of our faces, made him pause as if he understood what was happening.

"I'll uh, I'll catch the next one." He said backing up shaking his head.

Harmony who had turned when the doors opened now had her hands behind her back, in front of me; rubbing the front of my erection.

"Are we really about to do this?" she now questioned.

"It seems crazy, I know. But, sometimes you get tired of doing what you been doing and seeing the same ol' results. When you get the urge to go with your gut instinct, you gotta jump with both feet."

The elevator stopped again, I grabbed her bag along with my own and we both exited, walking in silence till we got to her room.

When she swiped the key, she opened the door for me to enter.

"Thank you."

I headed towards the window where the curtains were opened widely, sat the bags in the chair and was about to close the curtains till Harmony stopped me.

"Leave them open. The moon is shining brightly tonight and it looks so romantic."

I turned to see her sitting on the bed taking her shoes off. I walked over, kneeled down and began rubbing her feet.

Her toes were manicured beautifully, the Tiffany color blue. They looked like little candies. I massaged them for a second giving her the attention I knew most women desired but all too often lacked.

She reached down and rubbed my shoulders in quiet appreciation. There were no words spoken until I paused,

"Will you trust me?"

Without her having to respond I could see it in her eyes, her saying yes.

"You wouldn't be here if I didn't." she confirmed

"Stand up." I asked

Too often we forget to really take care of the person in our lives. The daily grind of everyday living kind of forces us to give a piece here or a piece there. We hook up when it's convenient and sometimes that's even rushed. As I looked within Harmony's eyes, I knew I wanted something different. I wanted to take a different type of chance. I wanted to turn her out not just sexually but in an intimate way.

She stood before me willing, as I unbuttoned her blouse. I watched as it hit the floor, moving to her bra next. I turned her around, slowly unhooking her. She rolled her shoulders back as I lifted the silky fabric from her body and dropped it too, on top of the shirt. I spun her around and looked at her breast. She covered them and looked away, which made me reach out and grab her chin; making her meet my eyes again.

I lowered my lips onto hers and kissed her lightly. I trailed kisses along her collarbone, down to the roundness of her breast. I cupped her right one and stuck my tongue out just enough to feel the hardness of her nipple. She hissed as I continued on to the next, gripping the other a little rougher this time. She reached out to unbuckle my pants. I stopped and pulled my shirt completely off and stepped out of my pants. I stood there naked, as she did the same.

I looked at her for a second, admiring her beauty and thinking about the hook to one of my favorite songs, *"Girl take it off for me, you know just what I want, it's always hard to leave, this private show..."* She blushed shyly.

I reached out to her, grabbing a handful of her hair and brought her back to me. She placed her hands on my chest and began kissing me, while playing with my nipples. I spun her around quickly, causing her to lose balance. Harmony caught herself on the bed, bent slightly over. I wasted no time spitting on my fingers and rubbing it on the head of my dick. I held her down with my hand and used the other to direct how I wanted her ass propped up. Without warning, I entered and we both moaned at the pure animalistic excitement.

I lost myself in this woman who I had just met. This woman, that for some reason I was drawn to. I couldn't explain why I felt as comfortable as I did but she had moved something within my spirit. I have never shared such intimate moments like this with any other woman in my life before. I never knew such feelings could exist as strongly, for someone I barely knew.

The love I felt myself wanting, was only expressed through stories and seen on movies. Almost immediately, our relationship had taken off. Harmony and I had become somewhat inseparable. I longed for her, when we we're apart. I reached for her, when I was in bed alone. Our beginning, I was certain not too many had. It was amazing when I reflected upon how God's mighty plan came to pass in my life behind a hotel reservation that had issues with clearing.

'Someone needed a thank you card.' I thought to myself still smiling at the thought of her. Had it not been for the mix-up, Harmony and I would've just went our separate ways. But fate brought that woman and me together.

It is a scary feeling jumping into an unknown situation with both feet, just going off of your heart. My mind at times creates these scenarios of doubt, plays on the fact that we don't know each other and that the pace we are going in is unrealistic. It plays on the behavioral patterns Harmony at times displays when she too I know questions the same thing. Underneath all of that beauty, I know exists a woman who has deep rooted issues with trust and with love. She is as scared as I am, however I know, she is my blessing.

I tell myself to walk in favor, and be to her what I know she not only needs but also what I've always wanted to have in a relationship. I can see she's so use to men only wanting sexual pleasures from her that anything else seems robotic, seems plastic, unsure if it's a trick or a potential set up to be let down. Harmony is guarded, and scared. I too am guarded and scared but I've been reassuring her that communication will get us through all doubt or uncertainty. I'm willing to do whatever is necessary to open this woman's heart to feel and open her eyes to see. She's deserves it.

****

Harmony

Tonight is the night. Quincy and I have a dinner reservation for 7:30 and I'm running so freaking late. I know he is disappointed. He always tells me "you're amazing Harmony just the way you are." I love that about him, always so reassuring. Who would've thought me, Harmony, would allow myself to love knowing how men abuse and take.

Hell has frozen over, but I feel I could love this man. I love the thought of him with every fiber of my being. He's showed me in such a small timeframe all sorts of things about myself I've never known. Or maybe I've always known I just didn't want to see it. He stripped away the layers of cold bitter steel that I embedded over my heart. He fought for my affection and love tooth and nail, he fought me…and won.

Knowing my reservations, I had for Kendall; I knew it would be best if I backed up from seeing him. He was smothering me and at times I felt I was being watched just by some of the comments he had made off the cuff. I did my best to put distance between him and I but it was still unnerving. The phone calls and the pop ups, it was like he didn't get the message. I thought to tell Quincy about it but didn't want to bring drama to him when he was so much a part of bringing about my newfound happiness. This was something I figured I'd handle on my own. I couldn't allow anything to get in the way of that.

My phone ringing snapped me out of my blissful daydream. The name flashing across my iPhone6 said "BAE." I slid my index finger to the right to answer it smiling at the thoughts of him.

"Hey, bae. I'm running behind, sorry. I know that you're gonna be beating me to the place but you shouldn't be waiting long."

"Baby yeah, you know your man is never late and is always impatient when it comes to seeing you. I'm like fifteen minutes away from the restaurant now." He responded

"You know I like to make sure I'm looking as good as I can be for my man, time got away from me."

"I love that you do that for me baby, but I'm always telling you that you're amazing just the way you are." He assured

"I know, but I want to do something special for you." I explained

"Make it special for Daddy now and I'll make it special later."

"Ooh baby you know I love when you talk that talk to me. Keep playing and we're gonna skip the restaurant and come back to my place and go half on a baby." I couldn't believe I said that but it just flowed.

We both chuckled, but new thoughts began to emerged. 'Would he want me to mother his children?'

"Bae you wild, but look hurry up and finish getting ready. The night won't go as planned if you're late baby, I have something for you. Ok?"

"Ok, ok, ok baby."

"I love you Harmony." he responded before hanging up.

I fell back onto my bed mesmerized by the words he just spoke to me. I never knew a love like this before and wondered if this was the feeling they described in movies or in books because I was like a little kid at the candy store. This man had become my everything.

I got up from the king sized bed and walked over to my vanity to apply some nude MAC lip gloss onto my lips. I stepped into my black off the shoulder slim bandage dress and placed my "So Kate" pointy toe pumps on my feet. I walked towards my wall mirror on the back of my bedroom door and admired how everything was fitting just right onto my body. I couldn't help but to feel myself.

'Bitch you slaying in that dress' I thought.

Hurriedly I rushed getting into the car and on the road not wanting to keep Quincy waiting any longer. It took me no time to get to the restaurant as traffic was light. As I pulled up I circled the lot twice looking for Quincy's car, but found it nowhere. Although I wasn't alarmed or anything, I just found it odd but dismissed it as him just probably parking on a side street or something. I strutted my 'I know I'm fine ass' to the door of the restaurant feeling as if I was Miss Beyoncé herself and immediately was greeted in a professional manner by the hostess.

"Good evening ma'am do you have a reservation?"

"Yes I do, the name is Quincy for a party of two."

"Oh yes ma'am we've been expecting you please follow me. The other party hasn't made it yet but I think you'll like what he has waiting on you."

"Oh wow. Thanks." I said a little bewildered knowing that I was the one running late and still I beat him to the restaurant.

As I began following behind the hostess I noticed we were walking on pink and white rose petals. I also noticed there were no other people around other than me the hostess and a few waiters standing by our table.

"Good evening, Ms. Harmony. Please, have a seat. My name is John and I'll be serving you tonight. Would you like to start off with something to drink until your other party arrives ma'am?" asked the waiter

"Yes, I'll take a water with a lemon wedge John thank you." I answered.

I wondered what Quincy had up his sleeve tonight. It was 7:45 and he still hadn't shown up.

'Let me try calling him' I figured. Quincy didn't answer. I called two more times back to back and tried to rationalize that maybe he got caught in traffic. It still didn't explain why he wasn't picking up the phone though.

"Hey bae I'm here, where are you sweetie?" I texted.

I waited a few minutes, looking down at my phone periodically, and still no response. I tried calling again and was becoming worried. I sat on edge listening to the phone ring in my ear, before the voicemail picked up.

"Hey baby it's me, it's now 8:15 where are you? I'm beginning to worry because it's not like you to not answer my calls or respond to my texts, please call me back when you get this." I spoke into his voicemail.

I was beyond worried but agitated that every so often the waiter would come to the table and ask the same damn question as if I was keeping him from something important.

"Would you like to move to another section or reschedule ma'am?"

In my mind I was trying to calm down but if he came near me one more time asking that dumb ass shit, I was going to fucking scream. I kept watching the clock on my phone and checking my messages but still nothing. I've called him over twenty times, and I just didn't know what to feel at this point. I was nervous, scared & upset. My mind started playing with me thinking that he stood me up but it just didn't make sense. 'Was this some sort of sick game where he came, got what he wanted, got me to lower my guards only to play me like a fool?' I began questioning in my head. This is exactly why it was hard for me to put my trust in men.

'You get fucking burned every time.' I was so fucking embarrassed.

The waiters I felt began staring at me like I was a fucking charity case. I grabbed my purse, left a $20.00 tip on the table and waltzed out of there the same way I walked in. Ain't no man gonna see me cry or act an ass I'm better than that. He just better hope I don't run into his ass anytime soon. I felt betrayed and heartbroken and that was just the beginning of the emotions I was feeling. I waited in that restaurant for two hours for that man. I called at least twenty times and sent him countless texts.

I called the local hospital and jail and came up with nothing. I didn't know what else to do but look at the open text message screen that had BAE going across and wish that there was a missed message or something that my phone didn't alert me too. The pain I was now feeling as my thoughts continued seeing the worst made me drive home in complete silence. All I wanted to do was get within the comforts of my own home, drink some wine and get through this night.

At 7:47am that next morning, my world came crashing down. I was awakened by a knock on the door. An officer standing in front of me asking if I knew Quincy immediately sent the worst pain through my body. I was frozen in shock as I heard Quincy was involved in a terrible car accident last night that left 2 people killed. They recovered his cell phone and used his call log to track my location being that I was identified as WIFEY in his contacts.

"Ma'am we will just need you to come down and identify..." the officers voice spoke before I passed out on the floor.

'Wifey... Wifey...Wifey.' I thought somewhere deep within my conscious

That's how they found me. They say he died instantly and felt no pain. I heard him say those words to me, but I didn't. I didn't want to hear that nor believe that he was gone. My baby was going to marry me, I knew it. That's why that dinner was so important to him and the reason why I should've been on time. My future is dead.

"Miss are you okay?" The officer questioned looking down upon me. I tried to get up but realized I was unable to. I screamed, hollered and hit my fists against the floor until my hands were sore. I felt arms grabbing me and I could hear talking, but it was all jumbled. I began to hyperventilate and panic. The reality that I would never see this man again started to hit me like a ton of bricks. I'm pretty sure my screams that bellowed from the pit of my stomach could've been heard around the block. I didn't care though. My heart and sanity died right along with Quincy in that accident.

****

On the day of Quincy's home going, another bomb was dropped into my lap that left me with so many questions. I'd seen a familiar face standing amongst the guest and immediately I became enraged. Politely dismissing myself away from Quincy's mother, I walked up on Kendall.

"You have no fucking right to be here, why are you doing this to me?" I said with a slight smile on my face so that onlookers wouldn't see how mad I was.

"Harmony, calm down, this isn't about you sweetie." Kendall said just as smug.

"I'm sick of you harassing me. I know you've been watching me by the things you have said and now you are here playing with my head. I want it to stop. Leave me alone!"

Kendall stood there in front of me with a smug look on his face. Without saying anything he shook his head and turned right when another disruption ensued.

"Why are you here asking me these questions now?"

I turned and seen two men standing by Quincy's mother. As I approached along with a few other people, I noticed the badges they wore on their belt.

"Ma'am we apologize, sincerely we do but new developments have arisen in this case and I just want to back track and make sure every t is crossed and I dotted." The detective said.

"This is very intrusive detective, you have to know there is a time and place for everything." I spoke up

"I understand but as you know time is of the esse-" he stopped briefly when the other detective whispered something to him. He held up one finger before speaking again.

"Harmony, correct?" he asked.

"Yes."

"Would you know of anyone that disliked Quincy or had any ill will towards him?"

"Ill will?" I repeated. This was a man who hadn't a malicious word to say about anybody. He was a hard worker and made the best out of every situation. He had his troubles I remembered him saying but he had said it was all about choices. We could choose to be victims of our experiences or we can be the victors and use them to catapult us to where we need to be. I couldn't imagine who would do such a thing.

"My son was a hard worker officer, very well respected. We haven't even buried my son yet and you come to his homecoming celebration with this? How dare you officer!!" Quincy's mother interjected.

"Again, I don't mean to upset you, I only want to get an accurate account of where he was that day."

"I only know of him going to work and planning a dinner date with me." I added

"Yes, detective and both Harmony and my son's employer are present if you want to question him as well."

"Where might he be ma'am?"

I too was curious to see who this man was that Quincy worked for. His mother looked around a second then pointed in the direction of the one person I never would've expected, Kendall. The detective thanked her for her cooperation and she went back to sitting down with other family and friends who were still paying their respects. I on the other hand was in a state of shock. This whole time Quincy knew Kendall, I couldn't believe it. I was getting sick to my stomach at the thought that this was a game somehow they played amongst each other.

I waited a few minutes till I seen the officers leave before I approached Kendall.

"Wait, how did you know Quincy?" I asked knowing but still in shocked by how I found out so casually.

"We worked together Harmony."

"That's it…you worked together, what…" He cut me off by walking up in my space so close that I could smell the turkey he must've eaten earlier on his breath. It was repugnant.

"For some reason you thought that you could dismiss me as casual as you would some trash by entertaining Quincy but you see how that ended for him. Wise up young lady, wise up." He patted me on my shoulder and walked away. I stood there for a moment shocked by his revelation and what it meant

'Oh my god, He…'

****

"Excuse me Ms. Turner, I've been sitting here listening to you for quite some time now and I must say your story concerns me. I can understand something like this being upsetting to you, however there are no records that you are this woman or if she even exists"

"My name is Harmony."

"No your name is, Leslie Turner. You have been here at this institution going on two years now."

"Lies! My name is Harmony and I know Kendall has something to do with this!"

"I apologize Ms. Turner but I do not know whom you are speaking of."

"Help me, he knows that I know that's why I'm here."

"What do you want me to do?"

"Let me use the phone to dial this number."

"I can't do that Ms. Turner."

"My name is Harmony and I am begging you."

There was a long pause between the two women where finally the clinician gave in.

"I'm sorry but that's against policy."

As the words sunk in, Leslie looked around. It was as if she was just noticing her environment for the first time. Immediately, she became hysterical to the point that orderlies had to come in and subdue her.

"Get off me, I don't belong here. Leslie is not my name!